what

they

found

what
they
found

love
on
145th
street

walter dean myers

WENDY
LAMB
BOOKS

Published by Wendy Lamb Books
an imprint of Random House Children's Books
a division of Random House, Inc.
New York

WENDY LAMB BOOKS and colophon are trademarks of Random House, Inc.

www.randomhouse.com/teens

Educators and librarians, for a variety of teaching tools,
visit us at www.randomhouse.com/teachers

Library of Congress Cataloging-in-Publication Data
Myers, Walter Dean.
What they found : love on 145th street / Walter Dean Myers. — 1st ed.
p.   cm.
Summary: Fifteen interrelated stories explore different aspects of love, such as a
dying father's determination to help start a family business—a beauty salon—and
the relationship of two teens who plan to remain celibate until they marry.
Contents: The fashion show, grand opening, and bar-b-que memorial service—
What would Jesus do?—Mama—The life you need to have—Burn—Some men are
just funny that way—Jump at the sun—Law and order—The man thing—Society
for the Preservation of Sorry-Butt Negroes—Madonna—The real deal—Marisol and
Skeeter—Poets and plumbers—Combat zone.
ISBN 978-0-385-32138-9 (alk. paper) — ISBN 978-0-375-93709-5 (alk. paper)
[1. Love—Fiction.   2. Family life—Fiction.   3. Beauty shops—Fiction.
4. African Americans—Fiction.   5. Harlem (New York, N.Y.)—Fiction.]   I. Title.
PZ7.M992Wgr 2007
[Fic]—dc22   2007007057

Printed in the United States of America
10 9 8 7 6 5 4 3 2 1
First Edition

For Spring Myers

contents

the fashion show,
grand opening,
and bar-b-que memorial service

When Daddy first came up with the idea we just all sat there crying our eyes out. We said we would do it, but I don't think anybody believed it at the time. He knew we were too upset even to talk about it, especially Mama. So the day I brought him tea and he asked me to sit down to talk about it, he got right to the point.

"Abeni, you and me have always been tight," Daddy said, sitting up on the propped pillows. "We've always had something special going on."

"I think so," I said.

"Look, the other day when I told your mama what I wanted, I tried to make it a little light because I knew she was going to be upset," Daddy said.

"It's hard to talk about," I said, feeling the tears welling up in my eyes.

"I know, baby, and I know your mama wants to do the right thing." Daddy's hand was shaking slightly as he brought the cup slowly to his lips. He sipped the tea, took a deep breath, and exhaled slowly.

"How you feeling?"

"I can hold things down a little better now that I'm finished with that chemotherapy," he said. "You know, what I wanted to do was to go over the things I said the other day and maybe tell you why I said them."

"About Big Joe's funeral?"

"Yeah, well, that was something," Daddy said. He smiled, but his face was drawn. "Big Joe giving himself a funeral while he was still alive gave me the idea. People still talk about that funeral and that little Puerto Rican gal singing. She's in college now, ain't she?"

"Out in St. Louis, studying journalism," I said.

"When I came to the realization that this cancer had won the last round, I started thinking it over—you know, adding up the pluses and minuses—that kind of thing."

"Daddy, you're going to get me crying again."

"Baby, I don't care if you cry, but I know I can count on you more than I can on your mama and Noee," Daddy said. "Your mama wants to see me off proper, and that's good. We're a churchgoing family and a homecoming ceremony is what everybody expects. But like I said before, I'm a black man who loves the three ladies he's enjoyed his life with. Noee ain't nothing but a child—lovely as she wants to be, she ain't got your spunk, Abeni. I guess you being the firstborn I wasn't sure what I was doing and halfway tried to make you into a boy."

"I'm all right as a girl, too, Daddy," I said.

"Well, can you see what I'm talking about?" he asked. "Can you see that this is a kind of gift I can give to my ladies?"

I tried to say yes but the tears were on their way and I was putting my head on his chest.

"I'll get it done, Daddy," I said. "I'll get it done."

A year ago my family had big plans. Mama had been working for twelve years in LaRose Beauty Salon and now the owner was retiring and my parents had put the money together to buy the business. "And we're changing the name to the Curl-E-Que!" Mama said. "And my girls will work alongside me."

We were all excited about opening up the shop, counting on Daddy's job with the bus company to keep us going while we built it up.

Then Daddy got ill and all the joy just drained from the family. We were close. Mama and Daddy had been married forever, and people on the block said that me and my sister were the most spoiled children in the neighborhood. That's how Daddy was.

"You start them strong and they don't go wrong," he always said.

I was strong. When I was young, Daddy, a big bear of a man, had me playing football and basketball and every other sport. I was tall like him, and big-boned. I liked to compete. Mama didn't know anything about sports, but she didn't mind me playing and loved to see me and Daddy together.

"Troy Evans," she would say, "you got the girl acting more like your little brother than your daughter!"

When Noee was big enough to go out and play, I thought we would be teammates, but she was different. Shy, big-eyed, and quiet, she was more of a watcher. Noee was happy just to be in the room with the family or, when we had dinner, to make sure that everyone had enough to eat. I had always been Daddy's girl. I felt terrible when we learned that Daddy was dying, but I felt good that it was me he was calling on to see to his dying wishes.

Daddy had said to us, "What I'm thinking about is the beauty parlor you've been talking about for so long."

"Troy, you don't have to worry about that," Mama started.

"Honey, the best thing that ever happened to me was to have a family to worry about," Daddy said. "You see these homeless guys hanging around the streets and some people say ain't it a shame that they don't have a home. What I say is ain't it a shame they don't have a family to take care of and be worried over. That's why I'm asking you to go ahead with your plans for the beauty shop and then make my ceremony something that's going to be special. If Big Joe can do something with a funeral, so can I."

But . . . Big Joe's funeral was fake. He said he didn't want to waste a good funeral on himself after he was dead, so he gave himself a ceremony while he was still alive. Daddy was right, people did talk about it. Some still thought it was stupid.

"Man don't have a bit of sense," Mrs. Lucas had said. "He's as cluck-headed as a one-legged chicken!"

I liked Big Joe, and after my father told me how much he was depending on me I went to Big Joe for advice.

"Now what does he want you to do?" Big Joe had one foot propped up on a milk crate as he sat in front of his apartment.

"He wants us to have the grand opening of the beauty parlor and combine it with his funeral and a barbecue," I said. "The fashion show part is my idea."

"And what Mama Evans saying about all this?"

"Just what he thought she would," I said. "She wants to have a traditional funeral for him. And I can see that as a sign of respect."

"Yeah, well, a lot of folks are going to be mad at you if you do like you say," Big Joe said. "Colored folks don't like to play around with their funerals."

"People in New Orleans have jazz funerals," I said. "I know we can pull this off. What I need from you is for you to come and say a few words if we can't get Reverend Glover to go along."

"You get it set up and I'll be there," Big Joe said. "Your father's quality people. Not many around like him anymore."

We bought the shop on May 15. We had a big sign over the store and a smaller one in the window saying, UNDER NEW MANAGEMENT. We took Daddy downstairs to see and he was so pleased.

Mama wasn't any good with the planning. She couldn't think about losing the man she had loved for so many years.

"Not a lot of black men can leave their families in good shape," Daddy said. "Me seeing my ladies with their own business, their morals intact, and three good brains between them is a blessing."

As Noee and I cleaned the store and painted it I could feel myself weakening, wondering if I could really make his dying a kind of celebration. When Daddy was taken to the hospital early one morning we were sure he wasn't coming home again.

"Bring me some pictures of the store," he said in the cab. "You know how to use that digital camera I bought you."

"He's thinking of everything to make this work," Mama said on the way home. "He's always been kind of foxy that way."

"He's pushing us," Noee said.

Yes he was, even from the hospital.

* * *

I called Micheline Curry and asked her if she would help with the fashion part of it.

"A high-style *funeral*?" she asked.

She wasn't living in the neighborhood when Big Joe had his funeral, so I had to start from scratch and tell her what my father had planned. She took it all in, but she still said she was skeptical. "I know he loves y'all and everything, but I can't imagine running a fashion show about what to wear at a funeral."

"That's not the point, Micheline," I said. "My father wants to promote the business and give us a running start. Making the connection with hairstyling and fashion is good for our image and good for you, too. How about something cheerful?"

"Yeah, well, okay," she said. "Let me think."

Daddy passed away in his sleep, quietly, on the fourteenth of June. We had a small private ceremony and then had the remains cremated. Mama was so tore up. For a while I didn't know if she was going to survive, herself.

"That's the only man I have ever loved," she said, over and over.

When I saw her face, the anguish in it, I remembered Daddy's eyes. I saw the same lost expression, the desperation as he knew he was going to be without the only woman he had ever loved. And I saw that what he was asking us to do, what he was trying to accomplish with this whole thing, was to reach over the boundaries and find a way of being with us.

Yes, Daddy. I can do this thing. I can do this thing.

I had already given the flyers to the printer. All he needed was the day and we decided two weeks after the cremation. We hired Skeeter and some of his friends to pass out the signs to the neighborhood businesses.

We expected some opposition and we got it. Big-time.

John Carroll called and told Noee that Sister Lucas was pitching a fit. I told Noee I would handle it if Sister Lucas brought her almost-bald self into the shop. Well, she did.

"If this is not the most disgraceful thing I have ever seen in this life I don't know what is!" she said, her eyes bulging and her little brown fist hitting the air for emphasis. "He was a good, God-fearing man and you sticking some advertising on his grave like he wasn't nothing!"

"Ma'am—"

"Don't ma'am *me*," she said. "We only live this life but once, and each and every one of us who has lived a Christian life deserves Christian dignity."

"Yes, ma'am."

Billy Carroll, John's son, came in just then. "Sister Lucas, this family has a right to do whatever they want and I'm going to help them get the word out."

Sister Lucas puffed up like a wet hen and her eyes began to bulge.

"And I like the ad card," he said.

Noee had made it and she'd done a fine job. Mama couldn't even look at it, and I know she had her doubts.

When the day came, I was worried. We hung streamers outside the shop, from the corners of the big sign to the pole that held the NO PARKING ANYTIME sign. I had practically begged Reverend Glover to come and he had only said that he would see what his time was like.

"It's Wednesday afternoon," he said. "I have a lot of business to attend to."

"What he means," Mama said, "is that he's going to sniff around to see how the land lies before he commits. I called him and told him just that and told him if he didn't come I would give him a piece of my mind that he didn't know about."

We borrowed folding chairs from Watson's Funeral Home and set them up in the waiting area, leaving an aisle for Micheline's fashion show.

Well, the first thing was that people didn't know how to dress. Some people wore black and others wore everyday colors. John Carroll, who owned the roti shop, had set up a hot buffet at the back of the room and we encouraged people to help themselves. As they ate everybody was looking at each other trying to figure out who was wearing the right thing.

We put on some Nina Simone, Daddy's favorite, and tried to keep it as light as possible.

Reverend Glover hadn't shown up by four-thirty so Mama got up and said, "Folks, thank you all for coming out to this memorial service for my husband. Troy Evans was my husband, my only husband and lover and best friend for forty-six years. He asked us not to be sad and not to be mournful with his passing, but to hold on to and be comfortable with the love he had for us when he was alive, and . . ."

Well, that was all Mama could say. She started crying and I thought that it was going to end right there with everybody quiet and whispering to each other the way they do at funerals. But then Curtis Mason asked, "Can I say something?" He was wearing his army uniform. Curtis had hit on me once or twice but nothing serious. He was his own person and I didn't know that much about him.

"Certainly, Curtis," Mama said.

He went up to the front just as Reverend Glover came in. Sister Lucas, in an old-timey hat with a veil on the side of her head, was with him.

"Did you want to say a few words, Reverend Glover?" I asked.

"No, I just stopped in to say hello," he said.

"Go on, Curtis," Mama said.

"Folks, I knew Brother Evans from when he coached

me in Little League," Curtis said. "He was always part of this community in important ways. All the youngbloods knew that if they needed some advice in a hurry they could always come to him and he would steer them straight. We knew he loved his family. One day I hope to be like him. I'm going back to Afghanistan and I don't know if I'm going to be all right or not."

"God will be with you, son," John Carroll said.

"But I know my block, my Hundred and Forty-fifth Street, will be keeping me in their hearts as well," Curtis said. "That's important to me, because if I get in the way of danger, I want to know that there's something I'm there for. Brother Evans was part of that. This business is part of that, too. I would personally like to thank you all for being here for Brother Evans because, in a way, I feel you're here for me, too. Thank you."

They gave Curtis a big hand and Reverend Glover went up and shook his hand. Sister Lucas got a smile on her face somehow. It halfway looked like she had a gas pain, but it was technically a smile. Micheline started the fashion show and soon everybody was eating and talking to each other and saying how good it was that a new business was opening. It spilled outside a bit and some winos came in looking for something to eat. John Carroll let them each take a plate.

When it was all over and me and Noee had cleaned up, Mama came over and gave us both a big hug.

"Abeni, Noee, your father is something else," Mama said. "I always knew he was smarter than me."

"Mama, how did you fix your mouth to get those words to come out?" I asked. "You know there's nobody smarter than the Evans ladies."

"Well, that's true," she said. The tears were coming again. Me and Noee were going to miss our father a lot. But not like Mama would. Somewhere in heaven he knew it, too. So he had set us up with a momentum that didn't allow too much looking back. He was okay, that man.

what
would
jesus
do?

"You going to have a whole row of hot guys on the wall?" Cheryl McKinney turned her head sideways as Mama Evans straightened the photograph she was hanging. "You want me to bring in some pictures?"

"Cheryl, these are all neighborhood boys, and some girls, who are in the military," Mama Evans said. "I'm trying to get some of the church women to write to them and send them care packages."

"I know two of them," Cheryl said. "That's Randy, who used to work downtown at the blouse factory, and that's Curtis, who got that little dimple in the side of his face. He is some kind of cute."

"I just hope they all make it home safe," Mama Evans said. "This war is working my one good nerve down to a nub."

13

"You know what I was thinking of doing?" Cheryl put her face as close as she could to the big mirror. "If you look real close you can see I have a few freckles."

"Well, a lot of light-skinned people with reddish hair have freckles, honey," Mama Evans said.

"You think I should have them colored? Maybe with some henna like I saw an Indian lady do on television?"

"Henna's a stain, but it comes off eventually, so if you really need to enhance those freckles—how many do you have? Six, maybe seven. It could work."

"Nine, but one might be a beauty mark," Cheryl said.

"Oh, I see." Mama Evans lifted Cheryl's hair and looked at the ends. "You haven't been pressing your hair with that strawberry gel you were using, have you? Because it looks a mess."

"No, ma'am, just touching up the ends," Cheryl said, settling in the chair.

"And what's this I hear about you and Evelyn not speaking to each other?" Mama Evans asked. "You girls have been friends for years."

"You remember that time we were in here and she was wearing that orange jumpsuit and had her tennis racket?" Cheryl asked.

"Yeah, I remember," Mama Evans said, brushing Cheryl's hair up from her neck. "That was the time you were going to change your entire style, and get back to your roots."

"Uh-huh, that's right," Cheryl said.

"I remember you said you were going to get some African braids, too—"

"On a Hundred and Twenty-fifth Street, so they would be authentic, too," Cheryl said. "You can get your hair done cheaper in Brooklyn but I don't think Brooklyn is really keeping it real. You know what I mean?"

"I guess so," Mama Evans answered, "but then you were going to have your braids dyed blond?"

"Uh-huh. I think those white girls in my school look so cute with their little blond African braids."

"Right."

"Then remember we were talking about her boyfriend, Martin?"

"Don't tell me you said something bad about her boyfriend?"

"I didn't say nothing bad about him even though he is a troublemaker. I even like his name," Cheryl said. "He's cute. Ain't no two ways about it, the boy is cute."

"He's an attractive young man," Mama Evans said. "How old is he?"

"Eighteen," Cheryl said.

"Then you and Evelyn left together," Mama Evans said. "I thought you and her were getting along just fine."

"We were. She was going to tennis practice," Cheryl said. "But I had just had my nails done over at the Korean place so I wasn't playing no tennis. I didn't spend all that money to get my nails broke playing tennis."

"Girl, you are really into your roots," Mama Evans

said. "African braiding and Korean nails. Go on with your bad self!"

"Anyway, we were walking up to the park and we started talking about Martin again. I said they looked like the perfect couple," Cheryl said. "She said that sometimes she wondered because when they walked down the street people turned around and checked him out before they checked her out because he was so fine. You know, Evelyn is sweet but she ain't no Foxy Brown."

"Okay."

"I said she didn't have to wonder about nothing," Cheryl said. "Love is love."

"Sounds good so far," Mama Evans said. "But how do you get from there to the idea of Martin being a trouble-maker?"

"Well, she's still going on about how she's not too sure because he's so good-looking and whatnot," Cheryl said, looking at herself in the mirror. "You know what I was thinking, too? I'm thinking I should get some highlights around my face to emphasize my eyes. What do you think?"

"That might look nice," Mama Evans said.

"So then I said to Evelyn, 'Hey, when he's making love to you and looking deep in your eyes, he must know he found himself something good.' And then she said that they don't be making love and looking into each other's eyes."

"Cheryl, that's kind of personal," Mama Evans said.

"No, it's okay," Cheryl said. "We're girlfriends."

"Still . . ."

"So if they weren't looking into each other's eyes I thought maybe he was into some freaky stuff," Cheryl said. "Which is all right with me because what people do behind closed doors is their business. But then she told me they didn't have sex at all. Nothing. Nada. No way."

"You know she's religious," Mama Evans said.

"That's what she started running down," Cheryl said. "But then I asked her what did she do when he started asking for some. She said they had an agreement that they would wait until they got married. She said that's what Jesus would do under the circumstances."

"Nothing wrong with that, Cheryl," Mama Evans said. "There was a time when people thought that waiting until you got married was what you were supposed to do. And many people still do."

"Those were the olden days, Mama Evans," Cheryl said. "This is today. You don't know what Jesus would be doing today. When you see a brother that pretty and he can get any girl he wants, and he's saying he don't want nothing even though he's in love, you got to start thinking about what could be wrong. Am I right?"

"I hope I don't see where this is headed," Mama Evans said. "You know you're letting your scalp get too dry. You can't just take care of the ends and keep your hair nice."

"A friend of mine puts green tea on her scalp. It's got antioxidants or something like that," Cheryl said.

"So I had to ask Evelyn did she ever think that maybe the brother is on the down low? Sneaking around and seeing men and stuff like that? She said that she didn't think it and she didn't believe it, and I could see she was getting into a huff."

"I wonder why!"

"I was wondering myself, Mama Evans," Cheryl said. "I'm just thinking about her. I know she didn't want to spend five years waiting for this dude and then see him running off with a man."

"Cheryl, people have their own lives and they have to deal with them as they can," Mama Evans said. "That girl was raised in a Christian home and she's trying to live what she's been taught."

"I know she's good people, Mama Evans, but how I know what he's up to?" Cheryl said. "I told Evelyn she needed to rub up on him a little and see how excited he gets. Then she could back off at the last minute if she wanted to, but at least she would know how interested the brother was."

"Or she could just take his word for it, Cheryl," Mama Evans said. "Relationships are built on trust."

"Uh-huh. But I heard about a guy who was married twenty-two years and had four children and then one day he woke up and realized he was a stone homosexual,"

Cheryl said. "He kissed his wife goodbye, left ten dollars on the refrigerator, and ran off with his mailman's cousin."

"Who must have woke up that morning and realized he was a homosexual, too," Mama Evans said. "Cheryl, I don't blame Evelyn for being upset with you. It's one thing to bring up issues and it's another thing trying to solve them when they're not really your business."

"She wasn't that mad with me, Mama Evans," Cheryl said. "She didn't get really mad until the next week."

"Sometimes it takes a while to think about a conversation," Mama Evans said.

"No, it was the troublemaker that got her mad," Cheryl said. "And he was the one that didn't know how to keep his mouth shut."

"Meaning?"

"Meaning I was not going to let my homegirl get her feelings hurt if this guy was not going to show correct," Cheryl said. "I knew I had to do something and do it quick!"

"Oh, Lord."

"I knew that if Evelyn was afraid to check the brother out I had to do it."

"You had no choice?"

"Right. So I thought that I would talk to him and just push up on him enough to check him out. So I got his number from Wayne who lives over that Egyptian store where they sell the loose cigarettes. I called Martin and told him I had to see him about something very important concerning Evelyn," Cheryl said. "I told him I was worried about her so don't say anything."

"Cheryl, please don't tell me anything I don't want to hear," Mama Evans pleaded.

"So he said he would meet me and I told him to come over to my apartment on Thursday morning at ten o'clock. He said he had to be in school at that time and I said—"

"Didn't *you* have to be in school at that time?"

"Yes, ma'am, but this was for my homegirl so I made the sacrifice," Cheryl said. "Anyway, I told him to come over if he really loved her. He said he would be there.

"He came over and I asked him if he really loved Evelyn and he said yes. Meanwhile, I had on my housedress and I was letting it fly open a little to see where his eyes went. They stayed right on my face and I wondered about that because most brothers, if they alone with a girl, will let their eyes wander all over the place.

"He asked me what was wrong with Evelyn and I kept stalling and telling him I didn't know how to tell him. He said he was going to leave and go ask her. I said if he asked and she told him they would probably have to break up. He kind of calmed down. Then I asked him to hold me because I was so upset."

"I know you washed your hair just before you came here because I can still smell the soap, but you didn't rinse it enough." Mama Evans took Cheryl over to the sink. "Did he go for you needing to be held?"

"No, and that made me wonder even more."

"Cheryl, some men are just wonderful and pure and trying their best to do the right thing," Mama Evans said. "You have to understand that."

"He said that he didn't understand how him holding me was going to help Evelyn," Cheryl said. "I asked him why he was just relying on his brain and what he was thinking. I told him that Evelyn was my friend a long time before she was his. So he broke down and let me sit on his lap. When I did I let my housecoat just fall open so he could take a good look."

"And he knew exactly what you were doing, Cheryl," Mama Evans said. "He's not a fool."

"I could see that," Cheryl said. "Which is why I went to plan B."

"Which was?"

"I told him the problem wasn't with Evelyn, it was with me," Cheryl said.

"Cheryl, please don't tell me you were going after that girl's man?"

"No way! How I look trying to steal somebody's boy-friend? As good-looking as I am I don't have to be taking no hand-me-downs!" Cheryl turned her head to one side and put her hand on her hip. "I have never been desperate for no man. But I needed to find out if this man was messing over my best friend. So I said it was about me and all I needed was to have him one time and I would be satisfied."

"I need some aspirins," Mama Evans said. "Sit under the dryer for a while, baby." Mama Evans dried her hands, switched on the dryer, and went for the aspirins.

The phone rang. It was Abeni asking if her boyfriend, Harrison Boyd, had called. Mama Evans said that he hadn't. As she hung up she looked at the photograph of her husband, Troy, on the wall near the shop's license. She wondered if he had ever experienced anything like the encounter with Cheryl.

"Okay, sweetheart, there you are gaming on your best friend's man." Mama Evans sat next to Cheryl and turned off the dryer. "Go on."

"So I took off my housecoat and my slip and asked him what he was going to do."

"What did you have on then?"

"Mama Evans, I was running out of ideas!"

"Yes, dear, but what did you have on?"

"I didn't have nothing on, and I did realize that it was too late to turn back. He looked me up and down and then he told me to sit down. I sat on the edge of the bed. Then he asked me what I was doing. Only, Mama Evans, he leaned forward and he looked so sincere that I told him everything that had gone on before. I told him about me and Evelyn being in here having our hair done. I told him about how Evelyn said she was in love with him and how I was wondering if he was, you know, the kind of man that liked other men.

"He took my hands in his and said it was a kind thing that I was doing. I told him to sit down because I didn't like having to look up to him and he sat right next to me. He started talking about how he didn't think I was the kind of girl that just messed around with anybody, and he was happy to know I really meant to keep him and Evelyn together.

"I told him that I knew I was sacrificing my body and everything, but since it was for a good cause it was all right and that he shouldn't feel bad about anything he did to me. He said I was one of the noblest women he had ever met. 'You are willing to make a great personal sacrifice to make the world a better place. Not many people are willing to do that. Most people just want to talk a good game but they don't want to get involved.'

"By this time I was feeling a little bad because he knew what the whole story was and going on about how wonderful I was and all the time I'm sitting there buck naked trying to keep my thoughts pure and it wasn't easy. You know when you're naked and talking to some boy you don't know that good, it's hard to concentrate."

"If you say so," Mama Evans said.

"So then he said I should put my clothes on and we could go out for a soda. I said okay and got dressed and then we went downstairs and over to the coffee shop and he bought me a double latte. He made me feel really good about myself, which most boys don't do, and I was even feeling good when he left. I thought it was over. He was sweet and he did love Evelyn, so I could see how he could control himself. That's when I found out he was a troublemaker."

"What did he do?"

"He went and blabbed to Evelyn," Cheryl said. "She came right over that night and yelled at me! I'm the noble one and sacrificing and everything and she getting all hincty. He had already told her that we didn't do any-thing . . . you know . . . intimate, but she was mad be-cause he had seen me naked and hadn't seen her naked. I said, 'Well, you can solve that real easy. All you have to do is—' "

"Cheryl, what is wrong with you?" Mama Evans shook her head from side to side. "The girl doesn't want to have sex with the boy until they're married, and she doesn't want to go around parading in front of him naked, either."

"He was the one that started the trouble," Cheryl said. "He could have just kept his mouth shut."

"And what would Evelyn have thought if you were the one to tell her that you had offered to solve her problem behind her back, and was sitting up naked on your bed with her man?"

"She'd be okay if she didn't jump to no conclusions, Mama Evans," Cheryl said. "And that's in the Bible. It says right there in . . . Judges or some place like that . . . it says don't be judging people and don't be condemning people. That's in the Bible. Really, it is. So she shouldn't even be mad."

"Cheryl, I definitely think you need some highlights around your face," Mama Evans said. "You need as much light as you can get, darling."

"That's just what I thought, Mama Evans," Cheryl said. "Ain't it funny the way we understand each other?"

mama

The alarm clock rang at seven and I turned it off quick. I knew Mama had been up mostly all night. Mikey didn't move so I went over and pushed him in the back.

"Get up and pee," I said. "You got to get ready for school."

I waited while Mikey sat up for a minute and then fell back down on the bed like he always do. When I pushed him again he swung at me and missed. Then he got this mean look on his face as he slid out of bed. I don't know how a four-year-old boy can learn to look so mean.

Mama hadn't opened out the couch. I looked at her face and it was a little puffy, but not too bad. Her arm was scratched up so I knew her rash was messing with her again. I could hear her get up in the night but I didn't hear her crying. That was good. I got the medicine from the jar in the refrigerator. She had enough for two more days. Then she had to go downtown to the clinic.

"Mama?"

She didn't move. I pushed her shoulder a little, not too hard, and she made a little noise.

"You got to take your medicine," I said.

"We got any juice?" she asked.

I said no, and she said she didn't feel too good. She had to take her medicine twice a day. It was already seven minutes past eight. Back in the room, Mikey was on the bed again.

"Get up," I said. "You got to go to school early. Mama's sick."

"I ain't going to school early," he said.

"You got to go early!"

"You can't make me go."

"Didn't Reverend Glover say we had to take care of Mama when she was sick?"

"He didn't say I had to go to school early."

"I'll give you seven cents if you go to school early."

"I don't want your old seven cents."

"What you want?"

"You make macaroni and cheese for supper?"

"Yeah, okay."

"I want eggs for breakfast."

"We don't have any eggs," I said. "When we move to

the big house we're going to have one whole room with nothing in it but eggs and bread and pickles in jars."

"I don't want no stupid pickles."

Mikey got dressed as slow as he could and I didn't say nothing, because I knew if I did he would just sit down and start running his mouth. When he first started preschool he liked it just fine, but for some reason he didn't like it anymore.

I put on my white blouse, the one with the red and brown birds on the collar that I liked, and my dark blue skirt and then white socks I had just found and washed. They were dry so I put them on and sat on the chair and looked in the mirror. They looked good and made me feel good. My knees were just a little ashy and I was going to put some Vaseline on them, but then I saw there was hardly any left in the jar. Sometimes Mama used it for her rash, even though it didn't help much.

Mama's eyes were closed when she threw a kiss in the air.

"You want to take your medicine before I leave?" I asked her.

"I'll take it later, honey."

Sometimes the medicine wasn't easy for her to take. It gave her a rash on her arms and her back and sometimes on her chest. My friend Jamal's mother, Mrs. Reed, said that the medicine also messed with the stuff Mama was taking to keep her off drugs.

"You get six parts of this and six parts of that," Mrs. Reed said. "And then you got to mix them all up and hope they keep your butt alive."

Mama was doing okay. She had stopped losing weight and stopped falling asleep when you were talking to her, but she wasn't doing perfect. Not yet.

I checked the calendar and saw the little red dot over the number. I had put the dots on the calendar to remind myself when there would be money in the Families' account. Mama said they were "party days." I hoped I wasn't wrong. Mikey walked down the stairs slow on purpose, just hoping I would push him or try to hurry him up so he could mess with me. No way. I went with him all the way to school and didn't talk to him at all. And I gave him some looks that let him know I meant business.

The thing was, I didn't want to have to spank Mikey. When Ronald, Mama's old boyfriend, was living with us he gave Mikey a beating that made marks on his legs where he had hit him with the ironing cord. I hated Ronald. I still do.

There were two teachers and a crossing guard standing in front of the school when we got there.

"You people are sure early," one of the teachers, a black woman, said. "How are you today, Miss Cummings?"

"Fine, thank you," I said.

Mikey said, "I'm not going to stay unless you stay with me."

"Then I won't make macaroni and cheese and I'll tell Mama not to buy you anything for Christmas."

"Poopy head!"

But he stayed. As I was going down the block I turned and saw him leaning against the fence. He looked real little.

Mikey looked small, but he was only four. As I walked along fast I thought about how if he kept growing and got twice as big in four more years, which would have made him the same age as I am now, he would be almost a giant.

The bodega on 138th Street is always the first store open that takes our card. Mr. Alvarez always says he shouldn't let me use it but he always does. On the dot day, the second Tuesday of the month, when there's more money in the account, the stores are always full. I went in and bought a dozen eggs, some chicken thighs, a loaf of bread, and a quart of orange juice. Mr. Alvarez rang them up, took the card from me, and swiped it through the machine. Then he handed the machine to me and I punched in our secret code, which was 0-3-3-5-2. I don't know how Mama came up with that number.

I was always a little nervous when I punched in the number because I was afraid that maybe there wouldn't be any money and we couldn't get anything to eat. Sometimes on the last few days, before the new money came in, we would be hungry.

Mr. Alvarez put the food into a plastic bag and I took it home. Mama was still in bed. I got her medicine from the refrigerator again. Her main medicine, the one she *had* to take, was in a plastic strip. You had to break it to push the pill out. I took one out and poured a glass of orange juice.

"Mama!"

She opened her eyes, saw it was me, and opened her mouth. I put the pill on her tongue and she made a face as she swallowed. She sat up and drank the juice. Her pills were big and sometimes she had trouble keeping them down. Once she had thrown one up and we had to find it on the floor and she had to take it again. That was yucky.

I felt better seeing that main pill go down. She had to take another one in the afternoon. It used to be six but now the doctor had cut them down to two a day. The other pills, the ones for the rash and the one because of her habit, didn't mean that much. They made her feel better, but the two main pills kept her from dying.

"I'm going to school," I said. "I put some eggs and bread and the rest of the juice in the refrigerator."

"There's money on the card?"

"Yes," I said, hoping she wouldn't buy a lot of stuff on the first day.

* * *

I was late, and Mr. Griggs pointed toward the sign-in sheet.

"You don't know what time school starts, young lady?" he asked.

"I know," I said, signing my name under the others.

He asked me my homeroom, gave me a late pass, and waved me on down the hall. It wasn't like I wanted to be late, and there were at least seven names ahead of mine.

Shakespeare, the class hamster, was loose and some of the girls were standing on chairs making believe they were afraid of him. Two boys had pointers and were trying to get him out from under the radiator.

"What are you doing?" I asked them. "You going to hurt him with those pointers."

"Why don't you shut up!" That's what skinny-faced Marva said.

"*You* better shut up before you get slapped!"

Miss Goldblum was sitting at her desk like she didn't know what to do. I crouched down on the floor, got Shakespeare, and took him back to his cage.

When the class came back to order Miss Goldblum started talking about how George Washington was elected as the first president of the United States. What she was saying was all right, but I started thinking again about moving into a big house. I had told Mikey about it so many times that I was beginning to believe it myself. Sometimes, when things weren't going well, I would make myself stop thinking about moving. Most of the time, though, I did think about it, and made plans to fix up a new place like the houses I saw on television. When I told Mama she said I was a mess but I could go on dreaming as long as I wanted.

Along with the big house I dreamed that Mama was all right and we didn't have to worry about things like her T-cells and making sure she took her medication. Everybody who knew what was wrong with Mama stayed away from our house. That made me feel bad, because being sick isn't something you should have to be ashamed about.

I didn't hear Miss Goldblum come up beside me, just some kids laughing. When I got back from thinking about Mama and the house I was going to decorate she was right by my side.

"Can you get your mind back to this class, girl?"

"Yes, ma'am." She didn't have to say that.

The rest of the morning went by slow but at last it was over. I was hungry. All they had for lunch was some greasy hamburgers, hard French fries, and vegetable soup. I can't stand no greasy food but I cut up the hamburger and put it in the soup. Then I found that the soup was cold. I ate part of it, though.

I saw Mikey in the lunchroom and waved at him and he made his make-believe gang signals at me. The preschool kids couldn't eat with the regular kids, so I couldn't talk to him.

When the last bell rang Miss Goldblum called me over to her desk and said that I had to write twenty-five times that I would pay attention in class.

"I can't stay after school," I said. "My mother is sick."

"You should have thought of that earlier."

"You can ask the principal, but I can't stay after school."

"I will do just that!" she said, and we walked downstairs to the office. She told the clerk and the clerk went in and told the principal.

"Mr. Griggs says to let her go," the clerk came back and told Miss Goldblum. "She's needed at home."

"Then you write it at home and you had better be on time tomorrow." Miss Goldblum was all huffed up.

I went on home and saw that Mama was still lying on the couch but the television was on. Yeah! That meant she was feeling a little better. It was almost three-thirty, so I got her other main pill and she took it with some water.

"Where's Mikey?"

I looked in our room and he wasn't there. Sometimes he hides in the closet, but he wasn't there either, and I told Mama I would go get him. Sometimes Mikey works my nerves something terrible. He's only four but he knows our rules. Reverend Glover explained all of that to him when Mama got home from the hospital.

After school Mikey is supposed to walk down the street to Frederick Douglass Boulevard, then make a left and come straight home. Sometimes he stops and plays on the way and sometimes he stops and looks in stores. He doesn't have any money so he can't buy anything, but he stops and looks anyway.

Now I walked over to the boulevard as fast as I could and then started walking uptown. I got one block and I saw Mikey sitting on a stoop watching some other kids play.

"Mikey! C'mon, boy, what you doing sitting here when you should have been home!" I said. "C'mon now!"

"No!" he said.

I hit him. I know I shouldn't, but sometimes he just has to listen to me and I don't have a lot of time to be explaining. He stood up like he was going to fight and I grabbed him and snatched him by the shirt collar. "I know where the ironing cord is!" I said.

He sniffled all the way home, and I felt bad, but I just didn't have the time to do everything right even if it meant I had to push Mikey around. And with Mikey, if you try too hard to do it right he'll try just as hard to mess it up.

I got home as soon as I could.

"Where were you, boy?" Mama asked Mikey.

"She hit me!"

"You needed it. You know you're supposed to come straight home."

That made Mikey mad and he folded his arms and

stomped out of the room. I like it when he does that because it looks cute.

The homework was stupid, just some easy arithmetic, some antonyms I had to write two times each, and a brief description of a place or thing. For my place I described a big house with a big door in the front and a little door on the side in case we had a cat.

Mama put some medicated powder on her back and chest, which was not a good idea because sometimes that made her itch worse than ever. I got her pill for her rash and she said that it wasn't helping too much.

"The doctor said that he couldn't give me anything stronger because it might affect my liver," she said.

Suppertime. There was some old grease in the refrigerator in a can and I put some in the big frying pan. I washed the chicken, then put some flour in the plastic bag it came in and rolled the chicken around in it. Then I put some salt and pepper on it the way I saw Mama do. When the frying pan got hot I turned down the heat and put the chicken in, one piece at a time.

I put on some rice and took out a bowl of leftover peas. I was going to wait until the chicken was almost finished and then just put the peas in the frying pan. Mikey came out and looked at the stove and asked me where the macaroni and cheese was. It had just slipped my mind.

I didn't want to go out again but I had promised

Mikey. Mama said she would watch the chicken and I went down to Mr. Alvarez and got a box of macaroni and cheese for a dollar and nineteen cents. If you have money, not just the card, you can get it at the ninety-nine-cents store for ninety-nine cents.

I made the macaroni and cheese for Mikey and we had supper. All during supper Mikey was holding his shoulder where I had hit him and saying how much it hurt.

Then we watched the news. Mama took her last pill of the day and asked me to put some lotion on her hands. I liked doing that and she knew it.

"Pat, don't rub," she said.

When I put the lotion on Mama we sat face to face and sometimes I just held her hand. We had a game to see who would smile first. Sometimes I would win and sometimes she would win.

Mama told Mikey to go to bed and he said he wasn't sleepy.

"Oh, good," I said. "Then I can give you a bath."

Mikey hated baths so he went to bed. When he gets into bed he always falls asleep right away.

I had forgotten about writing "I will pay attention in class" twenty-five times, so I did that. Then I was going to wash the dishes but Mama had already done them, which was a good sign. She was on the couch again. She hadn't pulled it out.

The television was on and I wondered if I should leave

it on. Sometimes if I turned it off it would wake her up. I thought about it for a while, and then I did turn it off. I pulled the sheet up on Mama so that it covered her shoulder.

In the room Mikey was making little noises in his sleep. I imagined he was dreaming about beating me up. I hoped he wasn't.

the life
you need
to have

"There's a man shortage in this school." Elena Rojas sat at a computer terminal in the Media Center. "There's maybe only one passable guy for every three girls. And, honey, I'm pushing it when I say passable."

"We're seniors," Gaylee answered. "Next year it's all about college and all the men are going to be at least passable."

"Maybe, but you know I read they got more brothers going to jail than going to college?" Elena had been scrolling through a site showing the different styles of African hair weaving and was just closing the page. "I'm thinking about putting an ad over the Internet. Wanted: Brother with something on the ball, must be anatomically correct with fresh breath—'cause I can't stand no man with stink breath—and a car."

"Girl, you are a mess." Gaylee started gathering her books for history.

"You still going away to college?" Elena asked.

"If I get a scholarship," Gaylee answered. "And I don't need a man to become a veterinarian."

"You hanging out after school or you working today?"

"Working."

They headed down the hall to class.

Mr. Siegfried's lecture on the feudal states of Europe went by easily, but the last class of the day was endless as the teacher droned on about the beauty of medieval English poetry. Gaylee gathered her books as the buzzer went off.

The weather was warm, bordering on muggy, as she walked toward the subway and her job at the Harlem Pet Clinic on 145th Street. Her mind was far away from feudal Europe and nowhere near medieval English. It was on Malcolm Boswell.

Malcolm was, in a word, smoking. Every girl at Baldwin High had checked him out from a distance and a few had even pushed up on the fine brother. He was a little over six feet tall with a sandy brown complexion and curly hair. To Gaylee, Malcolm's best feature was his eyes. Then there was that smile. It was an easy smile, not quite straight and not quite wide enough, but straight enough and wide enough to put a girl slightly off balance.

All of her sophomore year Gaylee had hoped he would notice her, but Malcolm had been too busy playing basketball and being the manager of the school's newspaper to pay attention to the tall thin girl with acne and an inclination to being slightly clumsy. But—and here came the good part—when the PSAT scores had been posted two weeks earlier for the junior class and Gaylee Brown's name had been printed in bold letters as one of the top three students, Malcolm had actually asked her to take in a film with him.

"This Saturday?" she had asked, squinting her eyes as if she were wondering if she was free Saturday. "Oh, all right."

She had been so excited she had sat in the Media Center and gone over exactly what Malcolm had said three times to make sure she had it right before she told Elena.

"He probably looked at you and was thinking to himself that you're pretty and you have class," Elena said. "You know his folks have money and they are *mucho* sophisticated."

"You think I should act super-classy or something?"

"Just be yourself, girl," Elena answered. "He came knocking on your door, baby."

Saturday came in a flash and Gaylee was impressed when Malcolm hailed a cab to go downtown. The theater was on Houston Street, one of those complexes in which they showed three foreign films and two American joints. Malcolm suggested they check out one of the foreign films.

"You don't mind subtitles, do you?"

"No," Gaylee said, even though she knew she would have to wear her glasses.

They were early for the film Malcolm wanted to see and found seats in the theater's coffee shop. While Malcolm was ordering two cappuccinos Gaylee started checking off her mental score card.

Malcolm had mentioned her test scores, which probably meant he thought her being intelligent meant something. Boys didn't usually like girls whose averages hovered near 3.6.

He had also not asked her to the mall, which could have been either positive or negative. For Gaylee the mall was a perfect drag. But maybe he just didn't want to be seen with her. Still, she *was* on a date, one of the few she'd had in three years of high school. Okay, the second she'd had during the three years. Ever. It all seemed good.

The movie was *The Fast Runner.* It was interesting, about an Inuit tribe and how they lived way up in the arctic regions. But the most interesting part of the movie had been when Malcolm took her hand and held it, both of their hands on her lap.

Malcolm's hand on her lap completely stopped her

from thinking about the movie. Later, when they had stood in the hallway of her building and he was saying goodbye, his smile pushing up her blood pressure as she leaned against the tiled walls, she was almost giddy with excitement.

He thanked her, brushed a kiss across her lips, and disappeared into the night, leaving her breathless and off balance. But he hadn't called back.

"I don't think I did anything wrong," she told Elena the following week. "I guess it was just a casual way for him to spend an evening."

"Track his butt down and cuff him!" Elena said. "You ever see how they catch those dudes on *Cops*? They follow every lead until they get their man and then they drag him away in handcuffs. As hard as men are to find these days, that's what you got to do, girl."

But Gaylee hadn't tracked Malcolm down. Instead she watched as he went about the business of being all everything and just a tad—was it possible?—better-looking. In the meanwhile she had concentrated on getting into the best college she could and had settled on Auburn, in Alabama.

"Why you going to Alabama?" Elena had asked. "You got people down there?"

"They have a really good biology program," Gaylee had answered. "And one of the best veterinary schools in the country."

"Did I tell you I was thinking of going to the University of Puerto Rico?" Elena asked. "Then I found out that you had to speak high-class Spanish and I decided against it."

The truth was that Gaylee wasn't that sure about Auburn, but they had offered her the best scholarship. She had completely shifted her thoughts to education and away from her nonexistent social life when the phone rang on a Wednesday evening in April at exactly seven minutes past eight.

"Malcolm," the voice announced in a smooth baritone. "Malcolm Boswell. How are you?"

"I'm good," Gaylee answered. "How are you doing?"

"Not sure," Malcolm said. "I think I'm going through one of those life-changing experiences. What are they called? Epiphanies? I was wondering if I could talk to you about some things?"

Yes! Sure! Of course, darling! she thought.

"Oh, okay," she said.

He asked her to go with him to the Studio Museum in Harlem. That Thursday they met in front of a large abstract sculpture that looked vaguely like a prehistoric bird flying over a black ball that could have represented the earth. Or something.

"So what did he say?" Elena asked later.

"Well, he said he was thinking about his life, what he really wanted and all, and what he was doing with it right now. He's been accepted to four colleges with a full ride to three of them. Did you know he had actually been thinking about Auburn?"

"Get out of here!"

"He said he applied there after he heard that I had. Later he started putting two and two together and remembering how good he had felt about our date and how he was thinking he wanted to go out with a girl who was doing something with her life."

"And that's you up and down, honey!"

"You know what he asked me? He asked me where I was."

"I thought you were sitting in the museum."

"We were," Gaylee said. "But what he meant was where I really was. He looked dead into my eyes and asked me where my heart was and I wanted to curl up and die. I mean, my heart was beating so hard I thought he could see it through my blouse."

"So, like, was he hitting on you?"

"No, Elena. Look, he's got to make a commitment to a school and he doesn't want to be too far away from me," Gaylee said. "And he wants us to be a couple. You know, Auburn is like a foreign land to me. There are no brothers going there who aren't on some ball team. I think he wants me to be his woman."

"He said that or you just thinking that?"

"He said he's had me in his heart for a long time, and now it's time he was accepting the feeling he had for me," Gaylee said. "I know it sounds romantic and every-thing, but I did ask him if he really meant it and he said he did."

"And he didn't hit on you? Because this is kind of sud-den, right?"

"Girl, you have a one-track mind. Look, I was think-ing, we don't have to be into a Romeo and Juliet kind of thing, but we can be supportive of each other and take care of each other while we're away from home. I'm not trying just to get a man or anything, but college can be hard and it's good to have some support."

"I think it's like when guys go into the army and they need to tighten up the home front," Elena said. "They get into settling down and stuff. Did he say he loved you?"

"No, but he said he felt we could be very special to-gether," Gaylee said. "And I have a lot of feeling for him. But I'm easing into it slowly."

"It doesn't sound that slow to me, Gaylee," Elena said. "But the brother is fine, so if you need to get on your track shoes—go for it. He said he had a lot of feeling for you, too?"

"He said that sometimes you find a special moment and you know deep within yourself that you have to rise to it," Gaylee said. "I think that's what it was for both of us."

"And what did you say?"

"I told him I would think about it," Gaylee said. "I think I'm going to call him tonight after I get home from the clinic."

"Call me up first and we'll make it a conference call and I can listen in and give you advice if—"

"No! I will handle the situation," Gaylee said.

At the clinic she was asked to clip the nails of a pretty Burmese shorthair. Gaylee wrapped the sleek animal in a fluffy white towel and took out one paw after the other to clip her nails as the cat purred.

"She likes it," said Dr. Van Pelt. "She gets pampered more than most people in this world."

"All of these animals do," Gaylee said.

"No, they don't," Dr. Van Pelt said. "Look at that shivering bundle over there."

Gaylee looked and saw the black and white patch of fur in the corner of an open cage. "It's afraid to come out?"

"Abused," Dr. Van Pelt said. "We've started antibiotics and cleaned him up, but we don't know if he's going to make it. He's dehydrated, but it's hard to tell how badly. We'll give him water for a day or so, but to save him we might have to hydrate him intravenously. That's a decision we'll have to make when we get to it. It's an expensive process."

"Who does he belong to?"

"No one, the police found him in an abandoned building tied to a radiator. He's a French bulldog."

"Why would anyone abuse a dog like that?"

"Gaylee, if you're going to be a doctor of any kind you're going to see abuse," Dr. Van Pelt said, leaning against the white cabinets. "People make up excuses why it's all right. They need to teach an animal discipline. They were angry. The animal misbehaved. In the end it's all about the unpleasant discovery that usually they can get away with it and move on to the next stage of their lives. We don't know who owned this poor dog."

"If no one . . ." Gaylee wondered what would happen next.

"Is he worth saving? Depends. Does his opinion matter? Do you think he wants to be saved? Finish the nails, then I need you to check out some turtles for a third-grade class."

"Yes, ma'am."

Gaylee finished the cat's nails, gave it a hug, and put it back in the visitors' cage to wait for its owner. All the while she thought of what she would say to Malcolm. She knew that the only word in her mind was yes, but she didn't want to seem too eager.

What, she asked herself, if Malcolm did try to hit on her before she went off to Auburn? Would she say yes to that, too? She closed her eyes and pushed the thought out of her mind. He had plenty of girls around him. She believed him. And, if worst came to worst, she would see what she would do when the time came.

"Since you have already left the premises in your mind, Gaylee," Dr. Van Pelt said, interrupting her thoughts, "you might as well go home now."

At home her mother was trying to get the ancient can opener to work and Gaylee chided her about getting a new one.

"You just need to get the can at the right angle," her mother said. "Oh, by the way, Elena called. She said it's important. You know, sometimes she has an accent and sometimes she doesn't."

"She thinks the accent makes her sound sexy," Gaylee said, scrolling through the numbers on her cell phone as she tossed her books across the bed.

"Gaylee?"

"Hi," Gaylee answered.

"Look, girl, I don't know how to tell you this." Elena's voice was husky and flat. "I spoke to my cousin Mimi and just mentioned that you were getting tight with Malcolm. She told me that Malcolm had a thing going on with Vanessa Josephs—you know her, she looks a little Indian or something and used to hang out with those girls who wanted to start a singing group? What did they call themselves . . . the Twilights?"

"What does this have to do with me?"

"Vanessa is like six months pregnant," Elena said. "I just thought you might want to check that out."

"That's his business," Gaylee said.

Elena was still talking, but Gaylee could hardly understand the words. She closed her eyes and covered her mouth with her hand. An image of a building being demolished on television came to mind. She remembered seeing the building shake, then collapse in a cloud of dust, the sky suddenly appearing where its silhouette had been.

Somewhere over the next minutes Elena was saying goodbye and Gaylee heard herself trying to sound cheerful as she said she would see her in the morning. Then there was silence, and then there was Gaylee falling across the bed.

That night Elena's words came to her again and again. Gaylee couldn't stop the tears or stop her hands from shaking. She thought about being in the museum, about Malcolm's quiet conversation, and what she hadn't said to Elena, that their conversation had ended with her taking Malcolm's hand in hers and holding it fast against her bosom.

"My heart is with you," she had said.

He had kissed her lightly on the forehead, and then, lifting her chin, had kissed her on the mouth.

Now she wanted to cry as a million thoughts ricocheted through the confusion that had been her mind. Suppose Elena was mistaken? Suppose she was just jealous and trying to break them up? But Gaylee knew Elena wasn't wrong. They had been friends for years and Elena had always been there for her.

After the museum she and Malcolm had walked through the busy uptown streets. There had been a breeze and Malcolm had put his sweater around her shoulders. They had walked and talked, with Malcolm saying that he finally knew what he wanted.

"I think I have a chance to do something really good with my life," he had said. "And I want to make good on that chance."

They hadn't spoken of love. There were no promises made, no pledges to be together forever. It was just Malcolm's feelings of needing to take charge of his life, to move upward and to find someone who could share in his thoughts.

"We make our lives," he had said.

"Yes," she had answered, still holding his hand. "We do."

It was nearly midnight when she dialed his number.

"I just heard something that I wondered about," she said. She saw herself gesturing in the mirror, as if it were some casual thing.

"What's that?" Malcom asked.

"I heard that Vanessa Josephs is pregnant," Gaylee said, holding her breath.

A pause. Gaylee thought she heard him clearing his throat.

"When I thought about what I wanted to do with my life," he was saying, "it was after I found out about

Vanessa. It was about doing the right thing for everybody, about not turning away from the life you want—the life you need to have—because there are detours.

"I think Vanessa and I drifted into a relationship without a lot of thinking going on. I don't think our lives should be that way—just sliding through our moments. Her saying she was pregnant was, in a very real way, a wake-up call, that moment of epiphany I told you about. I had to look deep inside myself and wonder what I really wanted from life. What kind of life I was willing to go for, and who I wanted to go with me on that journey.

"What I'm hoping is that you can forgive me my past errors and move on with me," he said.

Gaylee said she would have to think about it. She listened as Malcolm said that he would do right by Vanessa, that his parents would even help support her.

She felt that he was reaching for her, that he didn't want to end the conversation. What she wanted was to think, to run the words through her mind again, to hear them and weigh them.

But all she could do in the quiet darkness of her room was to cry. For a long time nothing else came. No ideas, no argument to be considered, just the tears and the disappointment.

She didn't sleep at all. She thought about Malcolm until the first light of day rose from between the redbrick tenements along Frederick Douglass Boulevard, and the

first rays of the sun began to glint off the windows along
the slowly waking street. Malcolm had had an epiphany,
a moment of suddenly realizing who he was and what he
wanted. Gaylee went into the kitchen and put on water
for tea. She needed to have her own moment.

She didn't see Elena for nearly the entire day. She had
seen Malcolm and he had asked if they could meet after
school.

"Malcolm, I'm a slow thinker," she had said. "I'm still
working on it."

"Gaylee, I love you," he had said.

She was at her locker when Elena came up to lean
against the locker next to hers.

"I should have kept my big mouth shut, right?"

"No," Gaylee said.

"You talk to Malcolm?"

"I can't look at him and say anything," Gaylee answered. "I know I'll just show how disappointed I am
and end up slobbering all over the place. You ever see
how bad I look when I cry?"

"Gaylee, I'm sorry," Elena said. "Look, I think he likes
you and doesn't care two cents about no Vanessa."

"Could be," Gaylee said. "But this morning when I got
up I realized two things. The first was that I was lonelier
than I thought I was and just hadn't admitted it to myself. The second was that after listening to everything
Malcolm said about fulfilling his potential and going on

with his life, I knew he was just talking about what he had decided to do, and what he could do. I'm not brave enough to spit out my two cents to his face, but I know I don't want to be his choice of the day. Right now I'm not in the mood for long explanations or even short good-byes, but I know I'm not going to see him again. So I'll just keep on feeling bad for a while and then I'll get over it. Look, I'm crying again."

"Oh, baby, I'm so sorry."

"Hey, so am I," Gaylee said.

At the clinic Dr. Van Pelt asked her if she was all right.

"You've been crying," the doctor said. "Is there anything I can do?"

"Not for me," Gaylee said, trying to force a smile. "I just wondered about that little French bulldog. You going to give him water through his veins?"

"You think he's worth it?" Dr. Van Pelt put down the manual she was holding. "We won't get any thanks for it. We'll lose money on him and he still might not make it. And with his tiny veins it won't be easy. But sometimes there just seems to be a right thing to do and you have to do it."

Gaylee opened the dog's cage and saw him raise his head, trying to respond. As she lifted the shivering animal out of his cage, her mind drifted back to Malcolm, as it did a hundred times a day.

He could have been the answer to a prayer she hadn't

remembered making, the fulfillment of a dream that had been too long in the closet of her mind.

"Don't get too attached to that dog," Dr. Van Pelt said, smiling. "If he makes it we'll probably end up selling him."

"It's all right," Gaylee said. "I'll be able to give him up when the time comes."

burn

I've always been quiet. Abeni said I was too quiet and shy for my own good, that I would never find a man if I didn't learn to "put myself out there." But I didn't have my sister's brilliant smile or that tough, tall body she inherited from our father. What I had was a heart always ready to retreat, eyes too eager to look down when a boy spoke to me, and a tongue that forgot how to speak when anyone expressed interest in me.

Between working in the shop, going to school, and volunteering at the Children's Center, I kept myself busy and pretended I wasn't interested in dating. Abeni told me I needed to come out of my ivory tower and give the boys a chance. What I wanted, what I needed, was for the boys to storm the gates and carry me off. I knew Mama was worried.

"Don't you think about boys sometime?" she had asked me.

I thought about them all the time. I just froze when they came near me. Occasionally I told myself that when Mr. Right came along things would be different. That's the reason I couldn't decide if I wanted Mama to know that I was *almost* having a date with Burn. Almost because when he had asked me out I had said no, but then I told him I was doing volunteer work on the weekend and we could always use some new volunteers.

"What you doing?" he asked, the dark eyes merely slits in his chiseled brown face.

"We're taking a boatload of handicapped children up the Hudson to Bear Mountain," I said, feeling myself look away from his gaze. "It's just a turnaround cruise. We pick them up in the morning and bring them aboard. Most of the day we play games with them or just let them watch the passing scenery, whatever they want. They have lunch on the boat and then we bring them back. It's a nice outing."

"Yeah, I'll come," he had said.

So in my mind it wasn't exactly a date.

"It may not be exactly a date, but it's Burn!" Mama was sitting in one of the chairs with her feet up and shoes off. "The man's a thug! What you doing with a thug?"

"We're not going out, Mama," I said. "We're going to Bear Mountain. Then I'm coming home and he's going wherever he's going."

"Noee, you haven't dealt with anybody like Burn before," Mama said. "And don't tell me what they haven't proven. That man is dangerous."

I had known Burn back in the day when he was Leon Robinson, a snotty-nosed kid everybody felt sorry for. His mother was caught up in the crack blitz of the eighties and he had to pretty much raise himself the best he could. There were stories about how the man his mother lived with had beat him, and how he had once lived in an empty apartment for days without anything to eat. Then, slowly, he had grown from a kid everybody pushed around into someone that everyone feared. He had been in gang fights and shoot-outs that made even the white newspapers, and had spent at least a year and a half in a juvenile detention facility. Now, at twenty-two, he was four years older than me but looked like he could have been in his thirties.

He had come into the shop a week earlier, with a sleek-looking white girl hanging on his arm. She was wearing a white jacket with a white blouse and a little black string tie, white silk pants that came down to mid-thigh, and a black lace skirt over the pants that came down to her knees. It was unusual but on her smallish figure it was looking good. She was built nicely and the only jewelry she wore were matching black onyx pinky rings and three diamond studs in each ear that looked fabulous. They made her blue-green eyes even more striking. She wore her dark hair up and wanted the back of her neck trimmed.

"I was going to try to do it myself using a mirror," she said, her Southern accent coming through strongly, "but I figured I'd probably just mess it up."

I trimmed her hair. She said her name was Sue Ellen and chatted about a letter from her father in Alabama. He was warning her about the dangers of New York, she said, as if Alabama weren't just as dangerous.

All the while Leon—now Burn—sat watching us. He had grown into a good-looking man, a little over six feet tall, and muscled. But the way he watched us, nothing moving except his eyes, he reminded me of a snake, and the whole world was potential prey. It was as if anything you said might set him off and he'd lash out. He wore a gold suit and a gold and black shirt open at the collar. He saw me looking at him in the mirror and smiled. I was embarrassed that he'd caught me checking him out and dropped my eyes to my work.

When I finished trimming her hair Sue Ellen paid me and gave me a twenty-dollar tip, which was more than the trim.

Abeni went to the window and gave a running account as they were leaving.

"He's got a driver who opened the door for Burn and she opened the door for herself," Abeni said, peering through the blinds. "And she made sure she showed some leg as she got in."

* * *

We talked about Burn and his lady friend for a while
longer before going back to the day's business. When the
door opened two days later and I saw him standing there
I was surprised. Mama and Abeni had gone downtown to
buy supplies and I was checking the bills. I knew he
wasn't going to do anything to me, but I felt a sense of
panic when he asked if we could go out sometime. That
was when the conversation ended with me telling him
about the boat trip.

I tried to put Burn out of my mind. I hadn't encouraged him in any way and he was smart enough to see
that I wasn't the kind of girl he usually dealt with. At
least I hoped he was.

Saturday morning. The late-August sun had burned
off the mist from the night before by the time I arrived at
the pier. The first cars and ambulettes had already arrived and the children were being escorted onto the boat
by either the Center staff or the volunteers. The children
were excited. I had been told that the youngest child
would be nine and the oldest a young adult as old as
twenty-one. Somehow they all looked younger.

The woman I was to work with asked me to help get
the lunch baskets aboard.

"I always feel that this is like the push-off for the inva-
sion of Europe," she said, smiling.

A lot of the children had cerebral palsy and were

either mildly or severely limited in their movements. Some were in wheelchairs and others used crutches. They used them well, too, I thought, as I struggled up the walkway with a stack of lunches.

I was hoping that Burn wouldn't show up. He would just be out of place and in the way. But on the way down the gangway I saw a gypsy cab pull up. He got out dressed remarkably sensibly for him, designer jeans and sneakers and a tight denim shirt that showed off his arms. I introduced him to some staff members as Mr. Burn and saw a smile flicker across his face.

He was all business helping the kids onto the boat and getting them settled. When the boat moved away from the pier he stood at the rail and watched as they waved goodbye to their parents and guardians.

We made sure that each of the children was comfortably positioned and gave them morning snacks and either juice or soft drinks. By the time the boat reached the George Washington Bridge I was already a little pooped.

"Why they so pale?" Burn asked, settling into the folding chair next to me. "I mean the white kids." Three-quarters of the younger children were white and the rest black or Latino.

"Because many of them don't get out all year," I said. "The Center works with them while they are in rehab, but after that it's up to other agencies to provide recreation. Sometimes their situations are really hard."

"Yeah."

Burn didn't say another word for the next half hour. He watched intently as the kids ate or played some of the games that the staff led. Occasionally he let his eyes drift toward the shore or follow the flight of the gulls following the boat for scraps of food. I thought I should at least talk to him. He was helping out and had worked hard. But I wasn't sure what to say to a guy everyone knew had been shot at least four times.

"I guess you decided that you wanted to be called Burn," I said.

A beat. "You think people would call me something I didn't want to be called?"

"I guess not," I said, "but why Burn?"

"It tells you where I'm coming from."

"Okay."

"Noee's a nice name," he said. "It's different."

"It's not really my name," I said. "My real name is Carol. When I was a kid I found out that there were two ways of spelling my name. Some people had an 'e' on the end of Carol. For some reason I didn't want them spelling my name wrong and that became more important than the name itself. So when people asked me my name—"

"You said no 'e.' "

I nodded and he smiled. It was a good smile, broad and open-faced. Then it quickly died and the face was hard again, a stone with eyes.

Two women from the staff joined us and the conversation somehow changed to being about whether the basketball players who claimed to be seven feet tall were actually that tall. Mrs. Polucci, a woman in her early fifties with a pretty face and beautiful black hair she wore loose, said she didn't believe they were.

"I think they just put out those numbers to impress people," she said. "What do you think?" She turned to Burn.

"They're that big." His answer was flat, dry.

Mrs. Polucci nodded uncomfortably. She switched the conversation to how lucky we were to have such a beautiful day for the outing.

"And thank you both for volunteering," she said a few moments later as she stood to leave. "We couldn't pull off these cruises without volunteers."

A thin Latino boy with a badge that read "Domingo" came over and asked Burn if he rapped.

"No, man." Burn spoke seriously. "How about you? You rap?"

Domingo put his head down and shrugged his shoulders. Burn reached over and pulled a chair close to where the youngster stood and pointed to it. Domingo had to turn sideways and kind of aim his body at the chair to sit in it.

"Let's hear you rhyme."

"I'm not too good," Domingo said.

"Yeah, but I'm not going to let you go until I hear it," Burn said.

Domingo rocked back and forth a little to get his rhythm; then he started his rap. It wasn't bad, or at least it made as much sense as most rap music made to me. Two other kids, a girl and a boy, came over and listened.

Burn's face didn't react to Domingo, but I felt he would have enough sense not to put him down.

"You're okay," he said. "You sound a little too much like Jay-Z used to, so you got to work on that. Maybe get you some new jams to listen to so you'll come up with some new ideas. But you're okay."

Domingo smiled.

"He's not a professional." The girl was weighed down with braces.

Burn turned and acted surprised. He asked Domingo if it was true that he wasn't a professional and Domingo sheepishly admitted that it was. Burn said that was all right, that he was still okay.

I was touched by the way he handled the kids and when they drifted off I told him that. No answer. No emotion on his face. He had turned back to stone, back to Burn.

"What do you do?" I asked him. "Just go around being hard all the time?"

He took a deep breath. A moment to think. "I work with what I got," he said. "Same as you. You got a good way of acting, you look good, you got a job. That's what you got to work with and you work it, right?"

"I guess so."

"So work with it," he said.

"Do you find . . . talking to children easier than talking to adults?" I said.

He just looked at me with a gaze that was so cold it nearly made me shiver. I swallowed hard and tried to think of something else to say. Nothing came. I didn't want to look away, to let him intimidate me, but I couldn't keep my eyes on his.

The trip up the Hudson toward Bear Mountain took four hours, and by eleven-thirty we were slowly turning for the return trip. Some other kids, probably ones who had heard about Domingo rapping to Burn, came over. He was easier with them than he was with the Center staff, or with me. He talked to them softly, asking them what they did in their spare time, what teams they liked. And he listened. As he spoke to them I saw how they edged toward him. Some touched his shoulder or his arm. I wished I hadn't made the remark about it being easier for him to talk to them than to adults.

I thought of the questions that Mama and Abeni would ask me about him when I got home. The truth was that I didn't know anything about Burn and I thought he didn't want me to know anything. All I understood was that I didn't feel comfortable with him, not like the kids did. But that was who I was.

The older children organized a video game contest and asked me to keep score. I couldn't believe how complicated their rules were and how fierce they were about sticking to them, but I did my best.

I found myself imagining that I was a child talking to Burn. Would he have kidded with me, made me feel comfortable as I vied for his attention?

Then I gave myself all the reasons I wouldn't want to be around him. But even then I knew why some girls could go for him. The whole hard thing, the stare, the short, almost grunted statements he tried to pass off as conversation. It was a huge male stereotype. Even as I told myself that I didn't need an ebony caveman in my life, I could see how it changed the whole man-woman thing. With Burn there was no give-and-take. He was the man and you had to figure out what that meant.

When the video games were over I found some shade and collapsed into a chair under an umbrella. The day had been more physical than I had expected, and the added tension of Burn had done a number on me. Mrs. Polucci and a perky young therapist from the Center brought over a pitcher of lemonade.

"I can judge the success of these outings from the amount of food consumed," Mrs. Polucci said. "They've eaten enough for a small army of crusaders."

"And we've only had one accident so far," added the therapist, "and that was a good one. A girl's legs folded under her and she couldn't get up. Then a boy who's more handicapped than she is tried to help her up and he fell down with her. Then two more kids just came over and plopped down and they all started laughing."

"What she isn't telling you is that she plopped down with them!" Mrs. Polucci said. "We had a little pile of people on the foredeck. I was thinking of making them all walk the plank."

"I spoke to your friend and asked him if he had enjoyed the trip," the therapist said. "He gave me a hand gesture that could have been yes or could have been no, so I didn't ask him anything more."

"He's being hard," I said, in my deepest voice.

We started talking about dream cruises we would like to take and were just about in agreement that we all needed to take an all-expense-paid cruise around the world when the first signs of the city appeared.

A yacht passed and the people on board, looking very fit and wealthy, held their drinks up in greeting. The kids waved.

I saw Burn headed our way.

"Why some of the kids upset?" He knelt next to my chair.

"They're not upset," I said. "Some of them are probably tired, that's all."

"They ain't tired," he said firmly, "they're upset."

"Burn, you know, these kids have had a long day and everybody is not as strong as you," I said.

"Mr. Burn, you're probably right about them being upset," Mrs. Polucci interjected. "For some of these children this is the one time in the entire year they get to be out like this. It's very hard for their parents to take them around. Today they're with friends, they're in the open air, and they're having a good time. When they see us returning to the city they realize . . . well, that their special day is over."

Burn grunted, turned on his heel, and walked away. Mrs. Polucci began talking about a plan that the city once had to check on the handicapped people and make sure that their lives were as full as possible. "But those great ideas run into funding problems."

There wasn't anything to add to that.

The boat slowed as we neared the pier. The row of ambulettes and buses lined up to take the children home looked like toys.

We started getting the children ready.

"We need to get your friend back here next year," Mrs. Polucci said, nodding toward a group of kids.

Burn had a boy of about ten on his lap. The boy was crying and a girl was trying to console him. I went over and saw how the boy lay sobbing against Burn's chest. Burn patted the boy's head gently. His dark eyes glistened as he held back tears.

This was something Burn understood.

Quickly I walked over to help some volunteers line up

wheelchairs and hand out what was left of the box lunches. There was a storm in my chest, a flood of emotions caught up in what I thought I knew about Burn and, perhaps, what I didn't know about myself.

"Can I? Can I?" A child in a wheelchair was looking up at me.

"Can you what?"

"Can I come again next year?"

"Yes, of course." I gave him a hug, ignoring the sticky fingers on my blouse.

Getting the kids ashore was hectic. Each of us was responsible for our own list of kids, making sure that each was delivered safely to their guardians or to transportation. It took nearly forty minutes before the last child was strapped in and waving goodbye.

I waited on the shore for Burn to finish with the children. Mrs. Polucci met him first and shook his hand.

There were things I wanted to say to Burn, but I didn't know what they were. On one hand I was so happy that he had been so good with the children, more sensitive to who they were and what they were going through than I was. He was not the simple person I had pictured him to be. On the other hand there was something about him that sent warning signals throughout my body. It was as if I had stumbled upon a rock and found that it had a heartbeat.

"You got any money?" he asked. "I gave mine to the kids."

In the cab uptown he was quiet, lost in his thoughts. I knew he was thinking about the children. I heard myself thanking him for being there for that boy. I told him I had been wrong about him, that he was different than I thought he was.

"There's more to you," I said.

I wanted to say that there was more to me, too. There was a me that could learn about who he was, that didn't mind how tough he was, or how hard he needed to be. I wanted to say words that my heart knew but that my tongue could not, somehow, pronounce.

The cab pulled up in front of the Curl-E-Que and I put my hand out timidly. He looked me in the face as he shook it. What he saw, through the hardness of the mask that had returned, was my own mask. If he had had the wisdom to put his head upon my chest he would have heard something deep inside saying I was afraid that I would be locked away for another year from a day like this.

"Goodbye," I called from the sidewalk.

He turned away and the cab eased into the late-afternoon traffic. For a long moment I stood on the sidewalk. I was confused, and hurt, and flooded with a thousand conflicting emotions.

When I walked into the shop, the tears were running down my face. Mama glanced up from doing the bills and a shocked look came over her face.

"Noee, you all right? What happened?"

"Everything," I said, "and nothing."

some men
are just funny
that way

"Hey, Keisha. How you doing, girl?"

"I'm all right, Mama Evans. How you doing?"

"Well, my arthritis and my high blood pressure are running neck and neck to see who's going to take control of my body." Mama Evans had taken down all the gels and lotions from the shelf to dust and was putting them back up. "And the tax people and the grocery store are running neck and neck to see who's going to take control of my finances. Now, other than that, I'm doing fine. What have you been doing with yourself? I haven't seen you for a while."

"I just dropped in because I need some advice," Keisha said. "And maybe a good lawyer."

"Did I hear somebody talking about a lawyer?" Abeni

came out of the back room of the Curl-E-Que with a styling comb. "What happened?"

"Well, I lost my boyfriend, I got a college scholarship, and I'm leaving home at the end of the month," Keisha said.

"I'm not too good on giving advice on how to get your boyfriend back," Mama Evans said. "Are any of these things connected?"

"You want to hear the whole story?" Keisha asked.

"I do." Mrs. Danforth was in Abeni's chair getting a touch-up. "Because I think her boyfriend left because she's going to have more education than he has."

"It's not the education, ma'am, it's the game," Keisha said.

"Go on," Mama Evans said.

"Okay, so Mr. Pearl—he trains the girls' team at Frederick Douglass—told me last week that this big-time white coach was coming to New York to talk to this Puerto Rican girl who plays for Powell."

"Keisha is a good basketball player," Mama Evans said to Mrs. Danforth. "She was in the paper."

"This girl from Powell is good, too," Keisha said. "And she's tall like Abeni, but Mr. Pearl wanted this woman to know about me even though our team didn't win our division this year."

"Did you beat Powell?" Abeni asked.

"No, but I was out sick that day," Keisha said. "I wish I had played."

"This white coach hadn't seen you play?" Mama Evans asked.

"No, ma'am. So the boys were having their tournament on a Saturday up at City College and Mr. Pearl set up a girls' game for eleven o'clock and invited this woman to come."

"Just to see you?" Mrs. Danforth said.

"Right. I show up and I'm all ready to play and Mr. Pearl said the woman hadn't shown up yet. There was going to be a boys' tournament at twelve, so we had to be off the court before then. Now if the coach don't show, there's no use in me playing."

"This white coach is a woman?" Mrs. Danforth said.

"Yes, ma'am."

"And your boyfriend was looking at her?" Mrs. Danforth asked. "I don't know why our boys love white womens."

"Will you let her finish her story?" Mama Evans asked.

"So I get in the game and I'm playing hard and the game isn't even serious," Keisha said. "Just a bunch of chicks goofing. Mr. Pearl is looking for this coach but she doesn't show. The game is over and she still wasn't there."

"You must have been disappointed," Mama Evans said.

"Not really," Keisha said. "I didn't expect nothing so it

wasn't a big thing. Anyway, I had some time to kill and I'm checking out the boys' game, which was kind of righteous because they had some fine-playing dudes on the court. Then Michael shows up and gets in the game. You know Michael, right?"

"I've seen him around," Abeni said. "He's tall, wears those rimless glasses?"

"Yeah. Well, me and him have been kind of tight."

"He the boyfriend you lost?" Mrs. Danforth asked.

"Let Keisha tell the story, woman!"

"So I'm watching the game and then Mr. Pearl comes up to me with this white woman and I knew this was the coach. I've seen her on TV," Keisha said. "She had those mean-looking eyes and tight little mouth like some white people have. But I know she's down with some b-ball. She said she had just flown in from Tennessee, but the plane had been delayed. She's smiling at me and saying how sorry she was that she didn't get to see me play and why don't I send her my clippings.

"I said I would, but my heart was still down. Since our school only won four games all year the clippings weren't that impressive. I knew that and so did Mr. Pearl. So even though that white woman was smiling and being nice I knew she was going to forget about me as soon as she left the park," Keisha said. "So Mr. Pearl went over to one of the older guys standing on the sidelines and told him what the situation was. Then he called me over and told me to get in the game."

"With the boys?" Abeni asked.

"These weren't just some boys," Keisha said. "Big Sal was there, Brian Addison was there, Jo-Jo Greene, and Footsy from a Hundred and Forty-seventh Street. You know, if my game is correct I can play with regular boys, but this was a coaches' tournament and there were a bunch of down dudes in the action."

"What did you do, honey?" Mama Evans asked.

"I jumped on in. Yo, it wasn't going to be easy but it's ball, right?"

Mama Evans nodded.

"So, it's me and Footsy—we're the silver team—at guard so everything is jumping off cool. Michael is on the gold team. I'm on the point and Footsy's playing shooting guard. We play off a few picks and I'm feeding the big men underneath and we're getting a lead. Footsy is helping me out on D and nobody is too anxious to go around me anyway because Big Sal is on my team and he's patrolling the lane big-time. So, I'm doing okay, relaxing into the set, and not only that, I'm having fun because boys are serious about their ball all the time."

"And this coach is watching?" Abeni said.

"Steady scoping!" Keisha said. "Then Brian—he's playing for the gold team—he peeps that I'm feeding off and he starts sagging and clogging up the lane so I have to start taking shots. Hey, I can shoot, so right away I hit a couple of outside shots and then the crowd starts getting in on the action because I'm a woman. They're saying things like 'Yo, she's busting you guys!' Footsy is digging it and he sets up a screen for me and when his man switches late I pop another outside shot. That's when Michael says he's going to hold me."

"Uh-oh, here comes trouble," Mrs. Danforth said.

"Please, ma'am, will you keep your head down?" Abeni asked Mrs. Danforth, gently pushing the older woman's head forward as she soaped the back of her neck.

"Abeni, you ever see Michael play?"

"No, I'm not into sports."

"Well, he's okay. He's not Footsy, and he's not Brian Addison, but he's okay. He's fast and he can get down on a fast break so he scores a lot when his team gets a turnover or a rebound. But when he plays defense he stands too straight. I tried to tell him that but he don't want to listen to me. He's one of these dudes who's good but don't want to work his game."

"Lot of men like that," Abeni said.

"Uh-huh. So he comes out on me and he's smiling. You know, I don't like people smiling at my game. You know what I mean? My game is not a joke so don't be showing your teeth. He's my old man—at least he was my old man—but he still had to show me some respect on the court. So he comes to me and fakes like he's going to snatch the ball and I guess I'm supposed to panic or something. I see how straight he's standing and how casual he's trying to look and I give him a head fake and go for his right shoulder."

"You hit him?" Mrs. Danforth asked.

"No, I just dipped my shoulder and went under his. You know, you get your shoulder past his shoulder and you go! So I cut across the lane. Brian thought I was going to pass and he cut off Big Sal so I was free for the layup. Then the crowd really went wild."

"Michael got mad." Abeni folded her arms.

"Mad? The fool started cussing and stuff. He come down the court and tried to post me low, which was stupid because, like I said, Big Sal done peed all over that inside paint. That was his territory and you better not step in it. So Michael is mad but he was still trying to nonchalant it on defense."

"And you weren't going to let that work!" Mama Evans said.

"My mama gave birth to a real girl and not some lame, you know what I'm saying?" Keisha had her hand on her hip. "So I went after Michael big-time just to reclaim my propers. First, I ran him into a pick at the top of the key and left him standing there looking stupid. I heard somebody telling him to fight through the picks, so the next time I had the pill I just pointed to the left and he looked for the pick and came straight up to slide by and I faked left and went past his left shoulder. He grabbed my T-shirt from behind but I pulled away, drew Brian over, and laid a pass behind my back to Footsy that was so sweet I wanted to run home and look for the instant replay on television."

"It was on television?" Mrs. Danforth asked.

"No, ma'am," Keisha said. "But that's what I was thinking. Michael's team called a time out and started strategizing. All the dudes in the stands started signifying and carrying on when the Golds came out and they had Brian guard me. That's a whole lot of respect because he's six foot eight and quick as a snake.

"The rest of the game was sweet. I only hit one more shot and one time I went up and Brian got my shot and pinned it against the boards but that wasn't a big deal," Keisha said. "Brian is liable to pin anybody. And by that time they had Michael sitting on the sideline."

"Please don't tell me he was still mad after the game?" Abeni was finishing up Mrs. Danforth.

"After the game Mr. Pearl took me over to the coach, who said she was going to write to the school for my records. 'If your academics are decent you'll be hearing from me,' she said.

"My academics are right in the middle but Frederick Douglass has a good rep so I was hopeful," Keisha said. "No way my moms can send me to college on what she makes. Anyway, last week I got the notice by telephone and a telegram."

"Baby, you got a scholarship?" Mama Evans wiped her

hands and put her arms around Keisha. "I'm so proud of you."

"Yeah! Now, I'm going to a mostly white school down in Tennessee, and I need some advice about how to keep my hair nice in case they don't have stores around there to buy the stuff I use."

"Girl, you are going to college!" Mama Evans said. "Anything you need for your hair you just let me know and I'll send it to you free of charge. And baby, Harlem is wonderful but they got black people everywhere in this country. You'll find some sisters down there who will definitely hook you up. Now go on and tell me more about this boy who's sitting on the sidelines pouting."

"So I ran into him on a Hundred and Forty-fifth Street and I told him—I said, 'Look, Michael, you were trying to be all cool and everything like I didn't even have a game! How you going to look me in the face and disrespect my ability?' "

"What did he say?"

"He said he would play me one-on-one any day in the week and burn me like I was a blunt at a roti-cue!"

"And what did you say?" Abeni asked.

"Well, you know me, girl. I really can't stand no shouting man and I can't stand no pouting man. So when a brother starts shouting and pouting at the same time I got to remind him of his place. So I did."

"You go, girl!"

"But Keisha, you said you needed some advice?" Mama Evans asked.

"About getting my hair together in Tennessee?"

"We got that straight," Mama Evans said. "But you also said you might need a good lawyer?"

"Michael said he was going to sue me," Keisha said.

"For beating him on the basketball court?" Abeni asked.

"No, ma'am, for hitting him on a Hundred and Forty-fifth Street," Keisha said. "I said I had to put him in his place. But when I started telling him about his stupid self—"

"Like you were supposed to—" Abeni said.

"He had the nerve to put his hand over my mouth. So I hit him. Mama Evans, I swear I didn't know his boys were checking us out. If I had known that I would have waited until we got off the block. I offered to help him up, but he told me not to put my hands on him and I would be hearing from his lawyer."

"Girl, you must of put a hurting on that man," Abeni said. "What did you hit him with?"

"An overhand right. He was standing too straight again. I still love him, though," Keisha said. "He's just hardheaded and got some kinks in his game. Other than that he's good people."

"Keisha, you pick out anything you want from here to take with you to Tennessee," Mama Evans said. "It's on the shop. You go on down there and make us proud. And don't worry about Michael. His ego's just been bruised a little. He'll get over it."

"Mama Evans, you are just wonderful." Keisha hugged Mama Evans, waved to Abeni and Mrs. Danforth, and left.

"I don't think that boy is going to get over being knocked down in the street," Mrs. Danforth said.

"I guess not," Mama Evans said. "Some men are just funny that way."

jump
at the
sun

I had slept badly, waking every few minutes to check the time. When I did sleep I dreamt of being lost in a large bus terminal, running from gate to gate trying to find my bus to somewhere. I was exhausted when morning finally came. I told myself that the strain of the last few weeks would soon be over, one way or the other. I was exhausted as I sat up. My head felt heavy in my hands and I wanted to lie down again, to sleep.

Snatches of conversation, all about the case, repeated themselves in my head. What had Frank Havens said? Oh, yes, that there was an outside chance that Donald would get probation.

"We made a good case for it," he said. His voice was high and tense. "Once we had Donald in the rehabilitation program things started to look up. The judge can see he's working on his case."

My brother was eighteen, two years younger than me, but somehow he seemed older. Our parents had spent the last few years trying to keep him out of trouble, watching in vain as he slid from small problems into the drug scene and, finally, an arrest for armed robbery.

Mama pushed the door open and held up a mug of coffee. I smiled.

"How you doing?" I asked.

"I'm scared," Mama said, sitting next to me on the bed. The sunlight through the venetian blinds fell in diagonals across her lap. "You can never tell about these things. He can get as much as twelve years. I can't imagine him being in jail for that long."

"We'll go into the courtroom today as a family," I said. "And we'll show the judge he has support. Mr. Havens said that sometimes the judge will allow the family to speak."

Mama rubbed my hands and said that she had to get dressed. "Donald went to Barbara's house to get his suit."

That was a good sign. Just last night he had been surly and going on about how the Man wasn't going to cut him a break because he was black and he didn't need to dress for the occasion. I had grown as angry as he was. Our folks had been putting up with him for the past few years, getting him out of trouble, begging people not to prosecute him for the petty crimes he committed. They had put up all of their savings to get him out on bail when he was arrested on the stickup charge.

Donald and a friend, Kwame Brown, had borrowed a gun and stuck up a gas station in Brooklyn. Kwame was the driver. When Donald ran back to the car with the money Kwame had panicked and taken off even before Donald was into the car. He had fallen on the sidewalk, and the gun had discharged. Luckily no one had been hurt. Kwame had been stopped two blocks down the road for speeding and had been arrested when the report of the robbery was sent out over the police network. Donald was arrested when he got to Barbara's, his girlfriend's, house. The robbery had netted them less than fifty dollars and now he was facing a possible twelve-year sentence. Kwame was pleading not guilty but Donald's lawyer thought that Donald would do best copping a plea and not putting the state through the trial.

"They have him on videotape," he had said with a shrug.

This wasn't the life I had imagined for myself, or for my brother. There had been a time when Donald had played high school basketball and was hoping for an athletic scholarship. We were going to be the first ones in our family to finish college and had made glorious plans for all the great things we were going to do with the stacks of money we made. Those days seemed so far away.

The sentencing was scheduled for eleven and we waited in the crowded corridor with several other defendants, their families, and a handful of lawyers. The court clerk came out and called people in as their cases came up.

"Where is he?" Mr. Havens looked at Mama.

I took out my cell and dialed his number.

"Yeah, who's this?" Donald's voice was deep, and raspy.

"It's Brenda," I said. "Where are you? Your case is coming up soon!"

"I ain't figured what I'm going to do," he said.

"You haven't . . ." I handed the phone to the lawyer. He looked at me and turned away with the phone cradled to the side of his face.

Mama grabbed my hand. Her eyes were panic-filled. I looked over at Daddy, uncomfortable in his blue double-breasted suit, and watched him turn quickly and fix his eyes on a portrait of some ex-mayor.

They were both beaten down. Numb. There had been too many times of getting up in the middle of the night to go to station houses or hospitals or wherever Donald turned up, too many prayers for God's saving grace and too many loans to pay lawyers.

Mr. Havens gave me the cell phone back and said that he had to speak to the court clerk. He went through the heavy wooden doors and Mama asked me what was happening.

"Donald is playing some kind of game, I guess. He said he didn't know what he was going to do."

"Didn't Mr. Havens tell him that he might get probation?" Mama asked.

"He knows that but he also knows he might go to jail,"

I said, immediately sorry I had made the remark. Mama didn't need truth, she needed compassion. "I think Mr. Havens is in there trying to get it straightened out now."

She was crying. I knew she would cry.

Mr. Havens came out and beckoned to us. "The judge is going to sentence him now," he said. "He's somewhere downtown. Said he's not coming. Nothing I can do except ask for mercy."

The court clerk called for my brother, pronouncing his name carefully and making a big show of looking at all the black men standing behind the wooden railing. Mr. Havens stepped forward and said that he represented Donald.

"Your Honor, Donald Griffin, unfortunately, is addicted to drugs and the family has been working with him trying to get him the medical attention he needs to beat this thing. This is a hardworking family, Judge. The father works for the city, the mother works, and his sister works and goes to college.

"He has been accepted into a rehabilitation program as the papers indicate. This is basically a good kid who's caught up in the drug scene."

"You also telling me he didn't show up today?" The judge, a roundish black man with rimless glasses, looked over toward us.

"Sir, Donald Griffin's family is here and would like to speak on his behalf—"

"Where is your client, Counselor?" the judge demanded.

"Right now he's sick and confused, Your Honor," Mr. Havens said. "I think he's having detox problems."

"He's got more problems than that," the judge said. "I'm going to give him a provisional sentence of thirty-six months and I'm going to suspend it for thirty days. If he doesn't show up within that time you're going to have to deal with his detox problems on your appeal. Next case!"

Mama tried to say something to the judge, but couldn't get the words out. Mr. Havens put his arm around her as we left the courtroom. He signaled me to stay behind when he left them at the train station.

"Look, Brenda, I can't stay with this case," he said. "Your parents don't have the money to pay me, and I can't afford to stay without pay. There are some good public defenders and I'll talk to a couple to see if one of them will take the case."

"You think he's going to end up in jail?"

His head bobbed from side to side as he searched for an answer. "I hope not."

He told me that Donald's not showing up forfeited the two thousand dollars my parents had put up for his bail. I wanted to go find my brother and beat his face in.

I asked myself, as I had a thousand times, what had gone wrong. It seemed that we had been doing well as a family, had been chugging along with clear goals and a straight path. I believed in the goals we'd set and the paths. I was going to be an accountant and he was going to be a physical therapist. That was how life was supposed to work for us.

I got home and Mama was sitting in the living room with the lights off. I turned them on and asked if she wanted me to make coffee.

"Did he call you?" Her voice was merely a whisper.

"No."

"I should have told him to stay here last night," she said.

"Mama, what Donald does is on him," I said. "It's not what you should have done."

"Your father's angry. I wish he wouldn't be angry."

"He has a right," I said.

Mama looked up quickly. I knew she wanted to see what I was feeling, if I was angry with my brother, too. The truth was that I couldn't be angry with him because I didn't know what was going on in his life. Disappointed. I was deeply disappointed. Whatever my brother did tore at the fabric of our family. Dragged it down. Made it bleed. I called him twice without getting an answer. The first time I left a message. The second time I cut the phone off when it clicked to the message mode.

We had all grown old in the last year. Mama's smooth brown face had begun to wrinkle, and little lines extending from the corners of her mouth had ruined her famous smile. Now I asked her to try to get some rest and she said she would.

I put on the coffee and sat at the kitchen table trying to think of what to do. What I knew, what I absolutely knew, was that there was nothing I could think of that Donald couldn't screw up. He hadn't always been that way. There had been a time when he was bubbling with promise and a joy just to be around. Family life had centered around him. Daddy had worked with him in Little League to teach him how to hit line drives and I helped him study to get into a good high school. Then he became a stranger, and I couldn't lie across his bed and talk to him for hours about anything, like I used to. Then came the drugs. It was as if someone had come to our house and had removed the plug that held in that sense of togetherness and joy that made us a family.

With the drugs came a whole new way of talking. Words like "tracks" and "possession" found their way into the living room. Words like "warrant" and "bond" were on papers my parents were signing on the kitchen table. The family bankbooks, which once had been hidden away with so much pride, were now kept within reach.

I decided to go to Donald's girlfriend's house. I had nothing new to say, nothing new to argue, but I took my jacket from the back of the chair and headed toward the door.

Barbara lived on Frederick Douglass Boulevard, between 134th and 133rd, in a five-story building they hadn't gotten around to rehabilitating yet. Two older men sat in the vestibule playing checkers on a board set up on a folding chair. There was a small baseball bat leaning against the wall and I knew they had appointed themselves protectors of the building, at least for the day.

"Hello, young lady." The dark-skinned brother looked up from the board. "What can I do for you today?"

"I'm looking for . . ." I realized I didn't know Barbara's last name. "My brother has a girlfriend in this building. Barbara something."

"Your brother a young man? Got a tattoo?"

"No, that ain't her brother," said the second man—he had once been big, but now his wide shoulders were betrayed by a thin, old-man neck and legs. "Her brother is that boy always got a starched shirt on. Go with that girl up there in thirty-one-G. Fifth floor. Name is Ronald— something like that."

"Donald," I said.

"Yeah. Yeah. I don't know if he's up there, but you can go on and take a look."

The elevator was slow and predictably foul-smelling, as if to warn anyone coming into the building not to expect too much. I wondered how children felt coming downstairs in the morning on their way to school.

When the car stopped on the fifth floor the door only opened partway—I had to push it open. The hallway was bright, with naked lightbulbs glaring from the ceiling.

Someone had put children's drawings on the wall facing the elevator with masking tape. I liked that.

As I knocked on 31G I didn't know what to say to Donald. Tell him that Mama was crying? Or that his father didn't need any more problems?

Donald opened the door with the chain on it, peeping with one eye into the hallway. The door closed as he took off the chain, then opened.

"Yo, what's up?"

My anger made me feel good. Who was he to come up with some hip-hop gesture of cool?

"Can I come in?"

He moved away from the door with a half shrug.

The place was a mess. I came into a narrow hallway strewn with old newspapers and a few articles of clothing. The kitchen was dirty. A row of empty jars next to the stained sink probably replaced their glassware. A small wisp of steam escaped from the teakettle on the stove.

"You want tea?" Donald asked.

"Sure."

He took out two cups and placed them on the table. He put a teabag in each cup as the kettle began to whistle.

"You remember we used to have tea when we were living on Edgecombe?" he asked.

I nodded. In the summertime, when our parents went to work, we'd pretend we were grown-ups and make tea and imitate our parents' conversations. Ages ago.

"Make believe I've already said all the things that you expect from me," I said. "Make believe I've already screamed about you not showing up in court this morning. I can't really get into it all again."

"I got to take Barbara to the hospital," he said. "She's sick."

"Glad you're thinking of her," I said.

He shot me a glance and I could see his jaw tighten and relax as he looked away. He drank his tea quickly, taking small sips, breathing deeply between each as if he were doing some sort of yoga exercise. When he had finished he stood and asked if I was going to wait until he got back.

"I'm taking her over to Harlem Hospital," he said.

Donald went into the bedroom and I could hear him talking softly. He was calling her name from time to time, even in the middle of a sentence, as if she were not paying attention, or falling asleep. I got up and went into the room.

Seeing her on the bed, the sheet twisted around one dark leg, her head bent forward, shocked me. She was having a drug reaction. I went to her quickly and put my hand on her forehead. She was warm. I shook her gently and she moved one arm. "Let's get her out of here!" I said.

Barbara was naked and I put panties on her as he dialed the emergency number. We tried to get some jeans on her, then settled for an old skirt and a blouse we found at the bottom of her closet. I asked him how long she had been like this and he said he didn't know.

"I woke up and started talking to her and she didn't answer. I just thought she was nodding out," Donald said.

"Nodding?" I turned to look at my brother. "Are you guys . . . ?"

"Using?" He straightened up. "No, I'm not using drugs."

Harlem Hospital was only a few blocks away. If you were stabbed, or shot, or going through an overdose, it was the place to go. They dealt with these emergencies 24-7.

The old men watched silently as Donald carried Barbara down the hall.

A light rain had started to fall as we hurried down the street. Donald was breathing heavily. Barbara didn't weigh that much and I wondered if he was having trouble, too.

The guard at the hospital looked up from his newspaper and pointed to the admissions desk.

There was no sense of hurry, no sense of white-suited angels of mercy watching a clock on the wall or doctors barking orders the way you see on television. It was just another young black addict in trouble.

Routine.

They admitted Barbara with studied casualness.

"She'll probably be okay." A light-skinned nurse rubbed her nose with one finger. "If they're stable when they come in they usually make it."

"What are you going to do tonight?" I asked Donald as we crossed the street from the hospital.

"Maybe I'll hang down here, in case she leaves the hospital tonight."

"Donald . . ." The tears started again, tears that were once inside and now came rushing to the surface. "Donald, you're killing us. I'm so torn up inside I don't know what to do. There aren't any answers, Donald. You got them damn drugs and they got you. They got Mama and your father and they got me. Don't you see that? Don't you see that?"

"Yo, Brenda, all that talk you're laying down is the real deal," Donald said. "But I ain't got nothing to say. Sorry ain't doing it. I know that. Promises ain't doing it. I know that. But I'm not doing what I'm not doing. You can't tell me nothing I don't know, but you can't tell me nothing that's going to fix the situation.

"Yo, check it out. Daddy used to say to me I got to jump at the sun. You know, reach for that good life. Well, guess what, big sister? I've jumped, and I'm not getting nowhere."

"Donald, you're killing us along with yourself."

"Brenda, what don't I know?" Donald's voice cracked. "What don't I know?"

I had wanted to see him sorry, to see him feel the pain

he was spreading around the family, but when I heard the hurt in his voice it shook me. It shook me because he was my flesh and blood. And because I had so few prayers for him that I thought God would answer.

"What are you going to do?" I asked.

"Maybe cop a hamburger, get some sleep," he said. "I don't know. You talking about saying something to Mama, but what am I going to say? You got something I don't know about?"

"Is Barbara helping you more than we are?"

"Naw, she don't help," he said. "But when I look at her face, I don't see the disappointment I see in yours."

The rain had just about stopped and I shivered. Donald asked me if my jacket was warm enough. I said yes, even though it wasn't.

"You want me to make you a hamburger?" I asked. "I can go over to the market and buy a few things. At least I can tell Mama you're eating. You want cheese? Sure, you always liked cheese."

He seemed embarrassed, and then nodded. "Maybe some fries?"

"And fries," I said.

He was talking and making sense. Everything he was saying was weighed down with feeling sorry for himself, but at least he was thinking.

There should have been anger. I should have been so mad I could have torn him apart. But I was past being mad. Past holding the fury in my heart. I told Donald what had happened in court. I asked him if he would turn himself in. He said he would think about it.

What I had to do, I thought as I crossed the street to the market, was to get him back to feeling that he was family again. He had to somehow understand that his feelings of frustration were what we all felt.

I bought hamburger, rolls, and onions. They didn't have any decent cheese so I bought the packaged slices. On the checkout line I called Mr. Havens and was surprised to hear him answer the phone. I asked him what could be done, if there was a chance for Donald to avoid jail.

"If he turns himself in within the next day or so," Mr. Havens said. "They've got so many cases on the calendar that they jump at a chance to clear one up. That's his best hope."

"And can my parents get their money back?"

"Something can probably be worked out," he said. "They'll be nasty about it, but something can be worked out. They'll get some of it back if he turns himself in."

So many cases, so many brothers. I found myself thinking like Donald. At first I tried to push the thoughts aside. Donald had been wrong in what he had done. That was his responsibility, not the rest of the world's. But I knew, too, that in my heart there was a difference between the world and our family. I could bring my brain to know what Donald should have done, but I couldn't change my heart and pretend that he was not family, my brother. I knew that somewhere, Barbara had family, too.

"They got you running tonight." The old man was alone at the checkerboard in the lobby.

"Sometimes it be's that way," I answered.

"Yeah, it do."

The apartment door was open.

"Donald?" I called. No answer.

I looked in the bedroom and he wasn't there. A moment of panic, and then I heard the toilet flush.

Back in the kitchen I washed my hands. Donald came into the kitchen. I had thought of a joke and decided to tell it to him. He had always liked jokes when we were kids. He would laugh at them even after I told them over and over again.

When I turned I saw him leaning against the wall. He had shot up.

"Yo, so you going to make a cheeseburger, huh?" His speech was slurred, his eyes were already half shut.

I didn't want to see him. I wanted to turn away and not recognize the slack-jawed figure, his body angled to one side, that slid along the wall.

"Why don't you go lay down," I said. "I'll call you when it's ready."

" 'Member when we had that Christmas party and we

had burgers?" he asked. He wiped at his cheek, as if he were trying to get something off it.

"Donald, go lay down," I said. "I'll call you."

Donald stumbled into the room and I imagined him falling across the bed. I sat at the kitchen table and let the tears come. They came in waves and in floods.

Donald was right. There was nothing to say, no logic to make things right. The drugs were his only logic, that and the pain he was dealing with. What was there to say when a person looked into his own soul and found it empty? What was there to do in the sad cubicle of Barbara's kitchen but to accept that the stained sink would never be white again, the scraped linoleum flooring would never look good, that there would never be fine glasses to replace the jars they drank from?

What I knew was that Donald had reached bottom. He was using again. It would be just a matter of time before he would be lying in a pool of blood on some street, or dead from the stuff he was buying to fill his veins.

The clock on the wall over the refrigerator said twelve past nine. It was later than I thought. At home Mama would be worried about me, and about Donald. Daddy would be asking himself for the millionth time whether or not he had been a good father.

I put the hamburger and cheese into the refrigerator. I looked in the bathroom. There were spots of blood on the toilet seat and, instinctively, I wiped them off. In the medicine cabinet were a hypodermic needle and two glassine envelopes. One was empty. I flushed the other one down the toilet.

I walked up to 135th and into the precinct. I gave the desk sergeant my name and told him that my brother was wanted by the police, and that he was at a friend's house and was high.

"Why don't you go get him and bring him down to the station?" he asked.

"No," I said.

There were more questions as I stood in front of the desk, unsure of myself, my nose dripping, the tears still running down my face into the corners of my mouth. And then there were two officers, one white, one black, going with me down the street, and into the tiny elevator. I hadn't realized how small it was.

They had me go in first. I sat on the bed at Donald's feet. He was still asleep. The cops rolled him over and handcuffed him before they woke him. They pulled him to his feet and he began to thrash around. The black cop pinned him against the wall and they patted him down. They found the needle, but nothing else.

By the time they had taken Donald into the hallway he had realized what had happened. He was cursing me. The names were vile, evil, as if they were coming from someone possessed. The black cop told him to shut up and Donald started cursing him. As we went out into the street all of my brother's demons were loosed upon the world.

"Do you need a lift?" one of the cops asked. I did, but I heard myself saying no.

I wanted to take my time getting home. What would I tell my parents? That Donald was back on drugs? Would that make his not showing up in court any easier? Would I tell them about how he had cared for Barbara? Would that make him any more human? Would I tell them that I turned him in? That they might get their bail money back? Would that make the pain any more tolerable?

When I got home they were sitting at the kitchen table.

"You okay?" Daddy asked.

"I'm okay," I said. "Just tired."

"We haven't heard from Donald," Mama said.

I went to her, kissed her lightly on the forehead, and said good night. Tomorrow would be time enough for mourning.

law
and
order

"Gates!" John Carroll put down his newspaper. "Ain't that Rudy just going past? Go bring him in!"

Gates got to the front door of the roti shop as soon as he could and called to Rudy. A moment later he was holding the door for the lanky, dark-skinned youth.

"Hey, what's up?" Rudy touched his fist to his chest and held it up in a black power salute.

"Yo, man, I heard you got picked up by the police," John said. "What happened?"

"I hate Arabs!" Rudy said. "They ain't nothing but a bunch of—"

"Yo, Rudy, don't bring no foul language in here over my food," John said. "What Arabs you talking about?"

"You know down on the corner where they be selling Lucys?"

"Yeah, fifty cents for a loose cigarette ain't correct," Gates said. "You buying a Lucy they know you broke from jump street. They should give you a break."

"Yeah, that's the place I'm talking about," Rudy said.

"So you were buying a loose cigarette and then what happened?" John asked.

"No, man, I wasn't buying no cigarettes," Rudy said, flopping down on a stool near the counter. "Let me have one of them meat pies."

"I ain't going to let you have none but you can buy one for a dollar," John said.

Rudy sucked his teeth and fished through his pocket until he found a dollar. He unfolded it carefully and laid it on the counter.

John gave him a curried chicken pie and a napkin.

"So what happened?" Gates asked. "He accuse you of stealing something from that raggedy store?"

"No, man, it's a long story," Rudy said.

"I ain't got no customers in here but you, so I got time to hear it," John said.

"Okay, I threw a rock through his window," Rudy said. He bit off one end of the pie and sniffed it before going on. "It didn't break the whole thing, just cracked it in the corner. I wished it had broke the whole thing."

"You must have been some kind of mad," Gates said. "I bet he used the 'N' word. You know Arabs don't consider themselves black."

"Gates, will you let Rudy tell the story?" John said. "Why you throw the brick through his window?"

"I kind of had to," Rudy said. "I had a problem."

"What did the A-rab do?" Gates asked.

"He didn't do nothing, but . . . okay, it's a long story."

"Rudy, you're getting me mad, now," John said.

"Okay, you know Angie White?" Rudy asked. "She lives in them houses near Marcus Garvey Park?" He set a dollar on the counter.

"Yeah, I know her," John said, putting a paper plate on the counter with a meat pie and a napkin. "Got a little knotty-headed brother always blowing snot bubbles out his nose."

"Yeah, yeah, that's her. Well, she was living with her moms and her stepdad," Rudy said. "Hey, man, ain't no meat in this pie, John."

"There's chicken in that pie, boy," John said. "Don't tell me how to run no restaurant!"

"Anyway, she didn't get along with her stepdad so she moved out. Then she joined a gang because she didn't want nobody messing with her. And she was supposed to get beat in."

"Beat in?" John lifted one eyebrow.

"That's when five people beat on you to see if you tough enough to get into the gang," Gates said. "If you start crying and ask them to stop then you too weak to get in. So if it's a girl gang, five girls beat on her until they get tired and then she's in. Ain't that right, Rudy?"

"Yeah, just about," Rudy said. "But Angie is tough so she beat the heck out of the five girls. I was there, man. She was steady kicking butt. She hit like a mule. One girl's nose was bleeding, one got a black eye, and one was just lying on the ground holding the side of her face."

"Sure sounds like a lot of fun," John said. "And y'all young people think that's cool, huh?"

"That's the way it goes if you want to get into a gang," Gates said.

"Anyway, one of the girls she punched out pulled a knife from her sock," Rudy said.

"That was wrong, right there," Gates said. "You ain't supposed to be doing that when you beating somebody into a gang."

"And the fighting and the black eyes were right?" John asked. "Why don't you young people just jump off a roof or something? Get it over quick?"

"I knew that wasn't correct and I called out to Angie—'Look out!' " Rudy said. "Give me another one of them pies."

"I thought they didn't have enough meat in them for you?" John said.

"Yeah, yeah, they okay," Rudy said, taking out another dollar and flattening it on the countertop. "Anyway, Angie told the girl that if she didn't put the knife down she was gonna kick her butt again and cut her.

"The girl—her name was Yovani, big cornbread-looking

chick—said she was gonna cut Angie. Angie kicked her on the leg and when she stumbled Angie hit her and the girl started swinging the knife. Only, you could tell that she was kind of scared of Angie. Long story short, Angie got the knife from the girl and had her down on the ground. The girl was crying and begging Angie not to cut her."

"She didn't cut her, did she?" John asked.

"Yeah, she did, but not bad," Rudy said. "She just cut her on the leg to let her know what was what."

"Lord, what is wrong with my people!" John shook his head.

"I think I know the secret to your pies, my man," Rudy said, putting half of a pie into his mouth. "It's the sauce. You using that Peri-Peri sauce from Africa. Right?"

"I make my own sauce," John said. "It ain't Peri-Peri, it's very, very hot. Now what does all of this have to do with the Arab selling Lucys?"

"Okay, so after the fight was all over and they had all got up and shook hands and everything—"

"Even the girl that was cut?" John asked.

"Yeah, it was over then, and Angie was in the gang so they all made up," Rudy said. "Then Angie came over to me and thanked me for warning her about the knife. And, you know, Angie is kind of fine."

"She's more than fine," Gates said, "she's got it going on!"

"Yeah, and you know I'm steady peeping!" Rudy said. "I told her I had been checking her out anyway, which was true, and I said maybe we could get together sometime if she was down for it. She said that was okay with her and she would see me around. Naturally, I got kind of excited behind that and the schemes and the dreams started flowing."

"I know what you talking about," Gates said. "She got a real nice face and a body like a model or something. Not one of them skinny models, either."

"Yeah, yeah."

"She even got some flow in her walk for a young girl," Gates said. "She's about—how old is she?"

"She's sixteen," Rudy said.

"So then what happened?" John took some uncooked meat pies out of the refrigerator and started laying them on a baking pan.

"So nothing happened right away because I didn't want to show up lame and I didn't have any money. My paper was so light I was down to reading yesterday's newspaper. You know what I mean?"

"So you're in your usual condition," John said.

"Yeah, yeah. But I ran into my homey, Billy Morgan," Rudy said. "And he told me he was going with his parents down to Howard University for the weekend. You know he's into books and school and whatnot. Then I remember when him and me were kids sometimes we used

to get into his house by going up on the roof and climb-
ing down between the buildings into his room and this
idea come to me—"

"If I listen to this part am I aiding and abetting?" John
asked.

"No, no, this is swift, man. I knew I couldn't just ask
him could I take Angie up to his place because he
wouldn't go for it. So I told him I wanted to know what
Howard looked like and figured he could tell me when
he got back. He said he was going to take some flicks
with his cell phone and he would show them to me
when he got back Monday."

"You didn't take that girl up there?" John sprinkled
chili sauce from a can onto the meat pies.

"Yeah, man." Rudy shook his head. "First I called the
house to make sure nobody was home. Then I went up
to the roof, came down on the fire escape, and tried his
bedroom window."

"They didn't have the window locked?" Gates asked.
"In New York City?"

"Billy's window has a lock on it but you can jiggle it
loose," Rudy said. "He never told his folks so he could
sneak out at night if he wanted to."

"So you're checking out your breaking and entering
skills . . . ," John said. "Go on."

"I've been in Billy's place a lot of times so I knew it
pretty good," Rudy said. "I open the front door and slip

a matchbook in the door so it won't lock. Then I bust over to where Angie lives and see she's hanging with her homegirls on the stoop. Then I asked her to take a walk with me and she said okay. We walked over to where Billy lives, just chatting and whatnot, and I asked her to come on upstairs."

"To Billy's place?" Gates asked.

" 'Cept I told her it was my crib," Rudy said.

"And what did she say?"

"Angie dug what was going down right away and said it wasn't no use because she wasn't going to do nothing. I made like I was shocked that she thought I was trying to get over with her. 'All I'm doing is treating you like my homegirl.'

"She kind of went for that but she was keeping her eye on me," Rudy went on. "I told her I just wanted to talk to her. You know, see where she was coming from. She said okay and we went upstairs. We get to Billy's place I took my keys out like I was unlocking the door, but it was already open and we went inside."

"You and this sixteen-year-old young lady?" John asked.

"She likes my pad—Billy's pad—and starts talking about how she wished she had her own place. So I got my arm around the mama and she's relaxing a little and I said let's go into the bedroom and we can just hold each other. I said we didn't have to take it no further than that. You know what I mean?"

"Yeah, and she do, too," John said. "Girls ain't dumb."

"Yeah, I know that, but she don't just want to put me down so she goes with me into Billy's parents' bedroom," Rudy said.

"She sitting on the fence!" Gates said. "She don't know what she wants to do."

"And Rudy wants to figure out which side of the fence he wants to come down on—felony or misdemeanor!" John said.

"So I'm checking it all out and I see she's thinking about what she wants to do, just like Gates is saying. On one hand I don't want to push it too hard because then I'll blow the whole thing but, on the other hand, you know . . ."

"You're not thinking with your head," John said.

"Yeah. Yeah. So, what I decided to do was to go into Billy's room and see if he had any protection lying around. I told her to wait for a minute and I'd be right back," Rudy said. "I go into Billy's room and I'm looking in his drawers for some protection when I hear some voices coming from the other room. First I thought she had turned the radio on. I'm listening, because if she's putting some music on I figure maybe she's made up her mind."

"Getting in the mood!" Gates added.

"But then it didn't sound like the radio, it sounded like people talking," Rudy said. "And I hear this scream!"

"Billy's back?" John crossed his arms.

"No, just his parents. And his moms walks in on Angie stretched out on the bed," Rudy said. "You know, it happened so fast I didn't even have time to think. Later, what I thought I should have done was to tell them that Billy said I could use the place."

"What did you tell them?" John asked.

"Nothing, man, I just split out the window."

"You left the girl?" John asked.

"So what she do?" Gates asked.

"Well, what I found out later was after Mrs. Morgan screamed her husband came running into the room and he saw Angie still sitting on the bed. She's thinking they're my peeps and trying to explain that everything is cool but Mr. Morgan went right to his closet and got his piece."

"He got a gun?" Gates asked.

"Yeah, he works security for the airlines," Rudy said. "Then—and I didn't realize how some people just don't want to listen to nothing—they called the police. That's how Angie got out to Rikers Island."

"She's in jail?" John asked as two customers came in. "Hold the story." He directed the customers to a table and gave them menus.

Rudy pushed all the crumbs together with a fingertip, scooped them up, and popped them into his mouth as John came back.

"Rudy, please don't tell me you got that girl in trouble and she went to jail?" John said. "I'm an old man and I can't take too much in one day."

"Yeah, man. That's how the Arab got involved," Rudy said.

"Okay, okay." Gates put his head down and turned his ear to one side. "Now run that by me real slow."

"Okay. Angie couldn't post bail so she got stuck in Rikers," Rudy said. "But the lawyer the city got for her convinced Mr. Morgan not to press charges and she copped to a misdemeanor of unlawful trespassing. She was only in two weeks and is just waiting for the paperwork to get straight and she's going to be back in the world."

"And the Arab is her friend?" John asked.

"No, man, but the word on the street is that she's going to be looking for me as soon as she gets out," Rudy said. "And I'm thinking about how she cut that girl just for pulling out that knife."

"You in a world of trouble," Gates said. "Angie was trying to get into that girls' gang, so she was being cool. She ain't going to be cool with you."

"I'm hip. That's why I got desperate," Rudy said. "You know she could get the whole gang on me. And you don't want to fight no girl gang, man."

"So why did you break the Arab's window?"

"To get myself arrested. I got to get off the street before she gets back to the hood," Rudy said. "She needs some time to cool down. What I'm going to tell her is that the cops were looking for me on another warrant and that's why I had to split on her. But she might not buy that too tough because I lied about it being my crib and all."

"Why didn't the cops arrest you when you broke the window?"

"That stupid Arab! That's what I'm telling you!" Rudy sucked his teeth. "Talking about how he don't want no trouble and he knew I was a good boy and all that kind of BS. Then he ran some of that Rodney King crap about can't we all just get along. And the cops don't care, either. When he put on his smiling and grinning and saying everything was all right act they just got back in their car and left."

"You can't depend on anybody these days," Gates said.

"So what are you going to do about the young lady?" John asked.

"In a way, I still got a lot of feeling for her," Rudy said. "I just need a way of expressing it."

"If she's as mad as she should be," John said, "and if she can fight as well as you say she can, and if she don't mind cutting no-account, lying lowlifes, you might try explaining yourself in a letter. Mail it from California, or some place like that. And let me ask you, Rudy. You learn anything from all this?"

"Yeah, I did," Rudy said. "You can't depend on either the cops or the Arabs to bring law and order to the hood. They unreliable. You should know what's going to happen if you break the law."

"Have another meat pie, son," John said. "Keep your strength up."

the

man

thing

"Eddie, I'm going downtown." Moms was standing in the doorway. "There's some eggs in the refrigerator. You awake?"

"Yeah, sure," I said. I had been awake, but hadn't got up the courage to start the day yet. "Yo, Mom, I got any shirts?"

"Over the chair in the living room," she said. "You going out looking today?"

"What else I got to do?"

She came to the doorway and threw me a kiss, which I pretended to catch, and said she would see me later. I listened as she walked toward the kitchen. Her footsteps were off rhythm and I knew her hip was probably bothering her again. When I heard the key turn in the lock I laid back down again. A few minutes later the ticking of the made-in-China clock on my dresser broke through the silence of the apartment. Fifteen past nine.

I got up and looked in my closet. I don't know why I was checking, I knew the gun was going to be just where I had put it.

"What else I got to do?" I let the words run through my mind again. The answer came through loud and clear. Nothing. I didn't have a thing to do except to get up, get dressed, and hit the pavement like a hundred other dudes on 138th Street.

It was funny but I couldn't even remember the days when there was always something to do, school to go to, a ballgame going on somewhere. Then one weekend everything changed. On a Thursday I was walking down the aisle at George Washington, picking up my diploma, beaming at the people who came to see the Class of 2005 graduate.

"Man, you're only seventeen and you copped your papers already?" My man Calvin Williams slapped me five. "You the man, bro, you definitely the man!"

But I wasn't the man. I was just another soldier guarding the sidewalks and the garbage cans on the street between Malcolm X and Frederick Douglass. It wasn't like I wasn't trying to find something, because I was serious about hooking up a job. A job was something I had taken for granted when I was in school. It was one of those step things. First step, finish school. Second step, nail down some kind of way to support myself. In the back of my mind I was thinking serious about hooking up my own crib, nothing too fancy because I didn't dig going into no whole lot of debt. Maybe I'd get me one bedroom, with a plasma box in the living room and maybe a DVD player. Yeah, definitely a DVD player.

But things didn't go smooth like I thought they would.

"So what kind of job are you looking for?" the woman at the State Employment Office had asked.

"Anything," I had said.

"We don't have jobs called 'anything.'"

She could sit behind her desk and come up with smart answers. She had her stuff going on, probably had finished college and heavy into a middle-class kick. Being black didn't even bother her. We danced that dance each week with her checking out her computer once in a while and sending me out one time to unload some trucks and another to do deliveries down in the garment center. Yo, I ain't proud or nothing, but I could tell the difference between a job that could get me started in the right direction and some work where I didn't count for nothing.

I spent six months staring people in the face and trying not to look too stupid when they asked me what I could do. Did playing ball count for anything? Did standing in the doorway and checking out the scene for three or four hours a day mean anything?

And nobody asked me about my high school diploma, which I carried with me. It was like it didn't even matter.

Things was getting worse because they weren't getting any better. I was getting up in the morning and knowing from jump street I wasn't going to find a job, and I would be coming home with my pockets empty. The routine of it just tired me out.

Then there was Moms. She was righteous. She didn't put any weight on me, but she was going downtown to Forty-fifth Street to clean in some hotel all day. Her with her hip so bad that some nights she had to sit up in a chair because she couldn't straighten it out.

I'm as deep as the next brother and I had definitely got down with the whole manhood thing. I thought I knew what it took and I knew I had the heart to play the part. But now I wasn't sure anymore. I had always thought of being a man as standing up for what you believed and not punking down if somebody got into your face. But even stronger than that was just plain old taking care of business when you needed to do it.

Then there was Little Eddie. Little Eddie is my son, and I always thought that one day I would get my thing together and hook up with him. If his mama was still correct maybe we could hook up, too. What was going to happen between me and her was one thing, but I always wanted to be there for my little man. In a way, he was getting heavy on my mind.

I went to the bathroom and peed. The sink in the bathroom wasn't working so I washed up in the kitchen. I thought about the eggs Moms talked about and looked in the refrigerator. Two eggs. Had she eaten? Probably not. I left the eggs and put on water for tea. While it was heating I sat at the kitchen table and closed my eyes, thinking about what had went down the day before.

When I ran into Pedro and Sheila on the Ave I hadn't been feeling great, but I wasn't feeling terrible, either.

"What you out here doing?" Sheila asked.

"Picked up a ball for my kid," I said, taking the ball out of the bag. "This Saturday's his birthday."

"How old is he going to be?" Sheila asked.

"Two," I said. "Seems like he was just born yesterday."

"And all you going to show with is a fifty-nine-cents ball?" Sheila asked. "Eddie, you got to do better than that, man."

That's when Pedro said that a day wasn't nothing but a day. Sheila wasn't that serious about what she was saying, but it still made me feel bad.

I remembered being little, older than two but little enough to think a birthday was special. My father had never showed for my birthday. He and Moms had never been married and he didn't treat me like somebody he cared for. But for some reason I used to always imagine him showing up with a wonderful present. It never happened. When I got older it didn't matter anymore. I dug my son big-time, and I wanted him to know it.

I knew Jeannie, Little Eddie's mama, would be cool with anything I did. She was good like that, but I still wanted to do the right thing. She had a smile in her voice when I called her and told her I'd be by for his birthday. Knowing her she would probably make a big deal over it.

Sheila walked over to a shop window and was looking at some hair products. That's when I told Pedro that she was not correct in what she had said.

"Why you going to let a woman mess with your head?" he asked.

"Her saying it wasn't correct because I don't need to be faced down," I said. "I would like to show with more than a ball but I'm running on empty."

"The kid's going to have a lot more birthdays." Pedro scratched at his little stubble of a beard. "Three weeks from now he won't even remember this one."

"Yeah, maybe," I said. "But it's not really about Sheila or even Little Eddie. It's like a man thing. You know what I mean?"

"Yeah." He nodded and looked down the street. "But check this out. You got all your life to be there for him."

Me and Pedro go back a long way. We went to school together back in the day when everything was about the future and what was going to happen. We were going to be ballplayers and astronauts and whatever and we couldn't wait to get started with the real stuff of life. I had hooked up with Jeannie in my sophomore year and she shared those dreams with me.

Jeannie was special. She made me feel that way, too. When I'm around her I just want to do more than I usually do and be more and even have a different look. We started hanging out and having fun. I liked to run my mouth and she liked to listen. That was important to me, her listening with that little smile and asking me questions about how I was going to do this or that. When Jeannie got pregnant it hit me hard because I wasn't ready to get married. When Little Eddie came I went to the hospital and seen him. I felt proud and happy, but at the same time I felt small.

There were some other fathers in the hospital and they were all talking back and forth and congratulating each other. A nurse asked who was Mr. Baker, and nobody spoke up.

"Aren't you Mr. Baker?" She turned to me.

"Yeah," I said, realizing where she was coming from. The other men started laughing, saying I was so shook up I didn't even know who I was anymore.

Baker is Jeannie's last name, and since that was the name on the baby's tag the nurse thought it was my name, too. I hadn't married Jeannie because I didn't have money for a place to stay or even to feed her. We talked about her coming to live with me and Moms, but we couldn't get help from the city if we lived together, so we decided to wait for a while and see what happened.

"It's a man thing," I told Pedro.

"I hear you," he said.

"Look, Pedro, you got any heat I can borrow?"

Pedro rolled his eyes toward me, looked away, and then turned to me and put his hand on my arm. "Eddie, you're not hard enough for nothing that heavy."

"I need to get paid," I answered. "If I'm not that hard then I got to get hard."

I tried to lay down a rap and it sounded lame, even to me. I heard myself telling Pedro about how I felt sick and needed some healing. In a way it was true. I was seeing myself fitting in with all the other dudes on the block standing around with nothing to do except waiting for their turn to fail. Some were hustling, some were dealing, and some were just giving up and copping whatever they could to ease the pain.

"Look, homey, I don't want you holding my piece because I don't think you're ready to go down that road and I don't want to have to take Noah's Ark to visit you on weekends."

Noah's Ark was what Pedro called the bus that went out to the jail on Rikers Island.

I knew he was just looking out, and when I pushed it he would let me hold it. I pushed, and he did.

I got the gun out of the closet and sat on the edge of the bed. I put the piece on my thigh. It seemed small, silver gray, dull. Dull like business. The thoughts kept running through my head, crowding each other trying to get my attention.

I thought of all the bad stuff that could happen. Somebody getting hurt, me getting arrested, a cop pinning me to the sidewalk while kids gathered around and pointed their fingers at me. I had seen this a hundred times. I didn't know anybody who did stickups that was successful. They all went down, if not the first time, then the next, or the next. Or the cops knew who they were and they had to get out of the city.

I'd never been in jail but I knew a dozen guys who had been. They tried to hype it like it was no big thing, but I knew it was. If life hanging on the corner was bad, then I figured what life must be like behind bars.

All the reasons to walk away from using the gun came flooding through me, including the fact that I was scared. Running into a joint with a piece in your hand wasn't easy. I thought of a dude I knew, I didn't like him but I had seen him on the block for years. He had gone into an appliance store and shot the place up. He killed the owner and a young brother working part-time. They caught him two days later hiding under his mama's bed.

After the trial and him being sentenced to twenty-five years to life, which is what you get in New York on a capital beef, some people from the hood asked why he had started shooting in the first place. He spit out some story but what they came back with was the dude had smoked a blunt to calm his nerves and it had blown his cool instead. This came to my mind because of the way I was thinking—scared big-time. I didn't want to hurt nobody. I just needed some paper bad.

After all the thinking and lining up all the bad things in my mind that could happen I was ready just to give the gun back to Pedro. Then I thought about what I would do for the rest of the day if I didn't do the get-over. I would just find my place on the block with all the other losers, like I always did. Maybe I would check down the street every once in a while to see if I saw Jeannie and Little Eddie so I could walk away.

When I was young and saw all the older men standing around, doing nothing, I used to look at their eyes. Empty. Nothing. Their eyes were empty. No "let's get ready to do something, to go somewhere." Just standing or sitting and waiting for whatever came stumbling their way. That wasn't what being a man was supposed to be about. You were supposed to be doing busy. Making something or working on some deal. Building a family and buying toys for your kids.

I started thinking about places I could knock off, places that had some paper around. The check-cashing place was fat, but I knew the brother who worked there was carrying a gun, and probably the owner, too.

I thought about the Curl-E-Que, but Noee might be there and she knew me.

The Arab store on the corner did good business but

that was too close to where I lived. Somebody might come in who knew me. Anyway, there were always three or four of them in the store, and I never dealt with Arabs before, so I didn't know what they might do. They might try to rush me or something and it would get into a shooting thing.

Once I heard two guys talking about the tailor shop on 132nd Street. The old lady there made curtains, put cuffs in pants. One guy was guessing that she had some money, the other one said he didn't think so because she didn't make that much, but he had never seen her go to the bank, so maybe she kept her money in the store somewhere.

I knew what the deal was. It was me figuring the old woman didn't have a gun and there wouldn't be any danger. It was me being scared. But I was weighing being scared, and maybe not getting too much money against fading away into nothing.

I looked out the window and saw that the day was bright. A few guys were in their shirtsleeves, some had on jackets. I put my jacket on and the gun in my belt. It felt uncomfortable. I hunched my shoulders and twisted a few times to see if it would move. It didn't, but I still worried about it falling out.

Vogue Tailors & Dressmakers used to be a barbershop. Outside there was a round plate in the ground where a barber's pole used to be. It was three doors down from the corner. Across the street was an empty building.

The windows had been boarded up and a tin sign had been nailed to the front door saying that it was for sale. The only people buying old houses in this part of Harlem were white people, and they were still downtown around 121st and 122nd Street. They hadn't got up to the thirties yet. I bought a soda and sat on the steps and checked the place out. The old lady inside worked at a sewing machine that was right up against the window. When I had passed by I could see she had a hot plate by her side and was drinking tea or coffee. I sat there for ten minutes, still feeling scared, touching my thumb against the handle of the gun in my belt, while I thought of how I was going to pull it off.

I would walk in and ask her if she put cuffs on pants and how much did it cost. Maybe I would say something about the weather. All the time I would be scoping the place out, making sure there wasn't anybody else there. Then, as calmly as I could and while I was sitting down so people on the street wouldn't see me standing over her, I would show her the gun, and tell her to give me the money and nobody would be hurt. Then I would make her lie down behind the counter and count to a hundred while I split.

Two brothers walked by. One was talking on his cell and I thought I would ask the lady in the shop if she had a cell phone. If she did I'd take it. I didn't need her calling the police before I got to the corner.

I was thinking about waiting until I saw a black-and-white pass on patrol. First I figured that if they passed once they wouldn't be back for a while, and then I realized I was stalling.

I walked across the street with the soda still in my hand. I wished I had left it on the stoop, but it was too late once I reached the shop.

A little bell rang when I opened the door. The woman was at the machine. She wasn't as old as I thought, maybe late forties, and small. She had light brown skin and dark hair with touches of gray around the temple. The kettle was still on the hot plate and I could see the electric burner glowing.

"Good morning," I said. There was a back room but I didn't see anybody through the open door.

"Good morning," she answered. "It looks like winter is waiting to come in."

"Yeah. Do you do pants?"

"Do you mean make them or put cuffs on them?"

"Either." Stupid answer. I sat on the chair next to the machine. "How much would it cost to have two pairs of pants made?"

She put her head down. At first I thought she was thinking, but after a while I wasn't sure.

"You hear me?" I asked.

"Please don't hurt me," she said. Her voice was so quiet I could barely hear her.

"I've got a gun."

"Yes, you have." She didn't lift her head.

I felt sick. I wanted to say something hard, to make her give me the money, but I was afraid to have her move. Suddenly my plans seemed stupid. If somebody looked into the store and saw her going behind the counter and getting down on the floor they would know she was being robbed.

I took a deep breath and let it out slowly. My hand was trembling and I put it against my side to steady it.

"I'm not going . . ." I wanted to say that I wasn't going to hurt her if I didn't have to, that I wasn't some kind of pervert. I felt myself getting a little panicky. How long had I been in the shop? A minute? Two? I should have been gone already.

"Are you all right?" she asked, looking up.

"Yeah."

A moment of silence.

"Would you . . . would you like some tea?" There were tears in her eyes. Her bottom lip quivered. She put her head down again. "Please don't hurt me."

I stood and she flinched. It wasn't what I wanted, what I had imagined. The door opened with the same tinkling bell. On the sidewalk two dark women, a shopping cart between them, spoke in West Indian accents. I took a long first step and started quickly down the street.

I crossed the avenue, looking behind me, looking for

the woman from the shop to appear at the corner, her voice screeching like the wail of a police car as she pointed a long brown finger in my direction.

Pedro had been right. I wasn't hard enough, wasn't cold enough to do what had to be done. I hadn't even asked her for money. I had just sat there, numb and scared and feeling sorry for myself.

The short walk to Pedro's crib took longer than it should have. My legs were stiff. Sheila came to the door and showed me in. I gave Pedro the piece and he asked me what happened. I noticed he didn't touch the gun.

"I chickened out," I said. "The woman I was going to take off got so scared it blew me away."

"Eddie, running steel is either you or it ain't you," Pedro said. He picked up the gun, sniffed it, then opened a drawer and put it away. "Carrying a gun is like hanging a sock full of cotton in your pants. It may make you feel good to show it off, but when the deal goes down, you can't pee through it. But some cats need that. You just found out what they spend their lives trying to learn."

As I left Pedro's place I knew that everything I had been thinking before was real. I was still black and poor and didn't have a thing to show for who I was except some empty pockets. I wanted to beat up on myself, or maybe get so high I couldn't think about nothing except laying down and going to sleep.

I knew what I was about. It was being a fake man. One

of them stick figures that little kids drew. Even with a gun it didn't make any difference.

I went up to Jeannie's house. She was still fine and she was only seventeen and didn't have but one baby. I was going to tell her she needed to find her another man. Maybe, if I ever got my stuff together, I could help her take a course or something. She had more going for her than I did, and if anyone was going to help Little Eddie it was going to be her. Like all the other baby mamas around the hood she was going to have to carry the load on her own.

"Where were you yesterday?" She stood in the doorway with a hand on her hip. "I'm telling your son you were going to show any minute and you don't even have the decency to call me! What's wrong with you?"

"Yo, Saturday's his birthday, right?"

"Yesterday was his birthday, Eddie!" The anger was all over her face. "What's wrong with you?"

"Man, look—I thought—Jeannie, I didn't have nothing to bring him and I don't think I'm—"

"Later for that noise!" Jeannie stood aside so I could come in. "That's your son. He's not interested in what you got out some store. You supposed to be here for his birthday and stuff. What's wrong with you? I'm trying to build you up so he can look up to you and you don't even show!"

"Yo, I'm sorry."

"He's in the bedroom," she said. "You go on in there and talk with him so he knows he got a daddy. And don't even *think* you're going to get next to me because you are not!"

I started to tell her that she couldn't tell me what to do, but she brushed me off with a wave before I could even get the words out. I went into the bedroom Little Eddie shared with Jeannie. He was sitting on the floor at the end of the bed pretending he was talking into Jeannie's cell phone. When he saw me he put a finger to his lips, letting me know I should keep quiet.

"Who you whispering secrets to?" I got down on the floor with him. "You got a girlfriend?"

He handed me the phone and I put my arm around him. He still couldn't talk too clear and I couldn't understand what he was saying but I knew it had something to do with the cell phone. Jeannie came in and sat down on the bed and watched as I played with Little Eddie. Once in a while I looked up at her and she seemed happy to have me there. I wanted to say something to her, to lay out the way I felt about not having nothing to bring to Little Eddie, about not being able to get a place for the two of us. But it all seemed like same old same old.

I hung for a few hours, then said I had to split.

"Where you going?" she asked.

"I don't know, to my moms' house, I guess."

"Lay here for a while."

"Hey, look, girl, I really feel bad not to show with nothing," I said. "No matter what you saying about how he wasn't looking for me to bring him nothing from the store. It still messes with me. You know what I mean?"

"What you think?" she asked. "I don't have a ring, I don't have your name. You think it don't mess with me? What I got is hoping that it gets better, that we'll be a regular family one day. As long as I see you're still acting like my man and Little Eddie's father I still got that hope and that's what keeps me going. Maybe you have to be a woman to understand that. What you think? You think a man can understand that, too?"

I sure as hell didn't want to, but I was crying. I was thinking about the women I had been dealing with all day—Mama, the woman in the tailor shop, and Jeannie. They were trying to hold their worlds together the same way I was trying to make mine.

"Dada crying." Little Eddie was standing, leaning against the edge of the bed.

"He's your daddy," Jeannie said, slipping her arm around my waist, "but I think he got some girl in him, too."

I put my arms around her and hugged her close. Then Little Eddie got mad at me hugging his mama and started hitting me. It felt good.

society for
the preservation
of sorry-butt negroes

"Honey, if you asked that smiling, charming, sweet-talking boyfriend of yours what a steady paycheck looked like he wouldn't have a clue." Maxine peered over her Armani glasses as she sipped a double latte. "He got Martin Luther King, Jr.'s message all wrong. Harrison Boyd does not have a dream, he's got a scheme. What do you need his sorry butt for?"

"Maxine, maybe you don't understand what it is to love a black man who has hopes that aren't that easy to come by," Abeni answered. "Sometimes you just have to have faith in a man. I think there will come a day when Harrison will definitely get over. And I want to be the black woman by his side that day."

"Oh, I get it." Maxine rolled her eyes. "It's a black thang

and I wouldn't understand because I'm not as black as you. Is that the four-one-one?"

"I didn't say you weren't black," Abeni said. "But check it out, Maxine, you're nineteen and you already have an associate degree, and you have a smoking job. Do you really think that life is that easy for every black person out here?"

"No, I don't," Maxine said. "But I know this. If I got my game together I don't want to be hanging with anybody who doesn't even have a game. And you, my ebony princess, are a fine chick. You're in college, pulling some heavy grades, and how old are you, twelve?"

"Going on nineteen."

"You're going on nineteen, you have a head on your shoulders, and one day you will own your mama's beauty parlor. So you're going to have your smarts, your business, and your sweet, sweet self. What do you need a sorry-butt Negro like Harrison for? He's just one of these smooth-talking dudes looking around for a crutch and thinking he's found one every time he sees a black woman. Two years ago he was going to start his own basketball league. Last year he was bringing in drugs from the Middle East."

"Rugs, Maxine, you know he was trying to import rugs for all the new apartments in Harlem," Abeni said. "And that was a good idea. It would have worked if he had spoken Arabic."

"Now what's he going to do?" Maxine tilted her head sideways. "Or doesn't it matter just as long as he's anatomically correct? Are you really that desperate for a man?"

"I am not desperate."

"Well, girlfriend, it's up to you. But sooner or later you're going to have to make up your mind about that man. 'Cause the way I see it, he's going to sweet-talk you into marriage, a bunch of cute little babies, and a long hard life before you wake up."

"Maxine, Harrison is okay, he just reaches a little too far sometimes," Abeni said.

"You need to be like your sister," Maxine went on. "That girl is into her books, working around the shop, and that's it. I've even seen her fix stuff around the shop with her tool kit, so she don't even need a man."

"Noee fixes stuff because she has a knack for it, which she got from our father," Abeni said. "And that has nothing to do with needing a man."

"Yeah it do, girl. That's God's way of telling her to keep her legs closed and her nose sniffing out slick-talking dudes like Harrison!"

It was hard to argue with Maxine. Harrison was twenty, had dropped out of high school three years earlier, and had been chasing one idea after the next. Somehow they all seemed good when Harrison was sitting in front of Abeni explaining how he would get rich if he just followed a few simple steps. Harrison was a big man, with a round face that made her want to smile when he came around, and you did not say no to those soft brown eyes.

Yesterday he had taken both of her hands in his, and with that low, sexy voice of his said, "The thing everybody is forgetting about is high-density cable. Brothers are out there buying some smoking sets and hooking up the high-density, but they're getting tired of having to watch reruns from 1970 and old movies that somebody's colored. What they need is some today television. Some short, hard-hitting pieces that speak to the African American community."

"And that's what you're going to be making?" Abeni had asked.

"Abeni, it can't miss," Harrison leaned forward. "You know what I'm thinking? I'm thinking if I can get you and your family to come in with me, we can bust in on the ground floor."

Yes, it had bothered Abeni to listen to yet another of Harrison's schemes. Nothing that Maxine had just said was new except for the last comments about making up her mind about Harrison. Abeni wasn't even sure how much she cared for him anymore. She knew she was tired of making excuses to her mother and hearing the jokes around the beauty parlor about Harrison's latest schemes.

* * *

It took her two entire days to run all of the issues through her mind, and might have taken longer than that if Harrison hadn't called her.

"I got to see you tonight," he said. "I feel something momentous is going to happen."

He got her to agree to meet him in the New Pam-Pam's restaurant across from Harlem Hospital at seven-thirty.

Abeni was tired, she had worked all day, had done four stylings from wash to set, and had "touched up" Mrs. Gunning's hair so that her bald spot didn't show.

"Do you think I should comb my hair straight back or to one side and maybe a little to the front?" The elderly lady looked at Abeni in the mirror.

"I just think if you keep your chin up and put a little dark powder on the top of your head your bare spot won't show so much." Abeni smiled back at her. "You've got nice eyes and you want to keep the focus on them."

Mrs. Gunning hadn't appreciated Abeni's suggestion and mentioned it to Mama Evans.

"She don't like it, but you were right," Mama Evans said. "I'll bet you the next time you see her she's going to have that chin up and batting them eyes all over the place."

Harrison was already in a booth in the New Pam-Pam's

when Abeni arrived. He held up his hands as if he were framing her in a shot as she made her way to the back.

"You have star quality," he said. "Some people have to work like a dog just to look presentable on film, but I think you have it naturally."

"Harrison, we have to talk," Abeni said, feeling more tired than she'd thought she was.

"Don't tell me your mother doesn't see the opportunity to invest in Abeni Studio Productions?" Harrison leaned back in his seat. "I just can't believe a woman that perceptive is going to let a chance like this slip by."

"I didn't even tell her about your filmmaking," Abeni said. "Because I don't believe in it myself."

"You *what*?"

"No, that's wrong." Abeni held her hand up before Harrison could interject his ideas. "What I don't believe in anymore is you. I think—I know—I need some serious distance."

"Abeni, honey, what are you saying to me?" Harrison asked. "You know I'm Harrison Boyd and I know you are Abeni Evans. So, knowing who we are, and what we mean to each other . . . go on and tell me what you are trying to say."

"What I'm saying"—Abeni hoped she would get the words out—"is that we—Harrison Boyd and Abeni Evans—are through. You need to pack up your ego and your dreams and go your way, and I need to pack up my ego and my dreams and go my way. I'm really sorry, but I have to make a choice about what my life is going to be about."

At least that's what Abeni told Mama Evans she said.

"And that's when he got down on the floor and started acting like a fool?" Mama Evans put down the jar of Miracle Gel.

"That's when he got down on the floor and started begging me not to leave him," Abeni said. "Everybody was looking at us."

"I know they were because Ethel—you know her, she got good hair on the top of her head and naps in the back—was in the New Pam-Pam's and she told Zinnia Lucas, and once you tell that girl something you might as well put it in the *Amsterdam News*. So what did you say?"

"I was too embarrassed to say anything," Abeni said. "Harrison is over six feet tall and weighs two hundred and thirty pounds, so you can't miss him."

"And he was crying, too?" Mama Evans asked.

"Mama, he wasn't like shedding a few tears, he was bawling and throwing himself around and crying so loud people from the front counter came back to take a look."

Harrison's getting down on his knees and crying so loud had shaken Abeni up. But it had been so embarrassing that she was speechless and didn't say one way or the other what she was going to do. People at the counter were looking at them and shaking their heads. Abeni took a deep breath and just looked at Harrison for a while; then she just got up and left. She called Maxine the minute she got into the house and told her what had happened.

"And I know you are not thinking about taking him back?"

"I don't know what to do," Abeni said. "I really think he loves me, even if his plans don't always work out."

"Don't always work out?" Abeni heard Maxine suck her teeth over the phone. "Girl, Harrison Boyd is just a dog like every other two-bit hustler out there. And don't come talking nothing about love to me. If you need some cute dude—and Harrison is not that cute—to support for the rest of your life go and adopt you a little Vietnamese baby or something. He doesn't need a woman, he needs a mama who can come around with a sugar teat in one hand and a checkbook in the other."

"I told him I'd let him know," Abeni said. "So I have to call him and tell him something."

"No, you don't! I guarantee he will call you and come up with some brand-new pitiful story," Maxine said. "He's supposed to be your man and you're the only one that can't see his game."

Abeni heard herself promising Maxine that she wouldn't

call Harrison, but in her heart she still wasn't sure. After all, Harrison was her boyfriend, not Maxine's. He might not have been perfect, but she felt she owed him something just for caring for her.

The phone rang again and Abeni thought it would probably be Maxine with some more advice. She looked at the phone display and saw that it was Harrison.

She was kind of thinking that if she and Harrison just cooled it for about six months maybe they would just drift apart and she wouldn't have to go through the drama of the split-up.

"Abeni, you in there?" Noee called.

"I got the phone, Noee," Abeni said. "Hello, Harrison." She tried to keep her voice impersonal.

"I need you to do it again." Harrison was talking fast again, his voice edged with excitement.

"Do what again?"

"Look, honey, breaking up with you was one of the biggest, most gripping moments of my life. I could feel myself going through changes. What I realized when I got home was that for the first time I had to reencounter my entire existence."

"And?"

"And what I knew I had to do was to relive that moment and put it on tape," Harrison said. "You know it's not usual when a person looks into the mirror of a moment and sees—I mean really sees—who he is."

"So what are you saying you want to do?"

"I want you to go through the whole thing again," Harrison said. "I know it was emotional for you, but that's all right. Life is really about emotions dressed up like ordinary activities. We think we're working, or riding the bus, but we're really in transit from one emotion to the next."

"So you want me to break up with you again?"

"I even spoke to Debbie up at Pam-Pam's and she said it would be okay if we didn't take longer than fifteen or twenty minutes to get it done."

"Whoa, wait a minute—"

"It means that much to me, Abeni," Harrison said. "Not as much as you mean to me, but this might change my life forever."

Abeni knew she should have said no, should have told Harrison that she didn't want any part of it, but she didn't. What had her friend Terry said? "That man must be loving your brains out." No, he wasn't, but they had been going together for enough years for some people to think they were already married. And it was true, Harrison could just about talk her into anything. She didn't have to call Maxine to know what their conversation was going to be like. But she did.

"Girl, he's trying to game you! He's been practicing some of his sweet talk and now he's going to get you back up into Pam-Pam's and run it up and down the aisle and he's going to have you backing up so fast you won't know what hit you. This is just one sorry-butt Negro who has got his own preservation society and that is you. And puh-leeze don't tell me that you owe him something because you're the only one giving anything."

If she hadn't told Harrison that she would be at Pam-Pam's at two-thirty and hadn't known that he had arranged for Debbie to give them twenty minutes, Abeni might have still backed out. She understood Maxine's point of view and had written down what she was going to say to Harrison, and told herself that no matter what he said, she wouldn't back down.

"Harrison, I have a serious problem with you," Abeni said, trying to ignore the video camera that Harrison's friend was holding and the lights arranged around the back booth in Pam-Pam's. "I just don't believe we can make it anymore."

"You don't believe . . ." there was a catch in Harrison's voice as he spoke. "Abeni, I thought you would always believe in my dreams. I thought you would always be there for me."

"I did, too," Abeni said. "But I just can't anymore."

"Baby, look, we—you and me, Harrison and Abeni—have meant so much to each other over the years. Knowing that—what we've meant to each other and how much I've loved you—what are you trying to say?"

"I'm trying to say—" Abeni felt terrible inside, and

ashamed, and embarrassed, but she was determined. "I'm trying to say we're through."

"You can't be serious." Harrison took her hands in his. "You can't look me in the eyes and say—"

"We're through!" Abeni said, looking Harrison Boyd directly in the eyes.

"Oh, no!" Harrison's head snapped forward into his outstretched hands.

A woman across the aisle gasped and spilled her coffee. A teenager took a quick step backward as he saw Harrison's entire body start to shake. The sobs were heartrending. When the big man looked up, his face was already streaked with tears.

"Please . . . baby . . ." Harrison's lips moved but no other sound came out. Then he put his head down on the table again and seemed to twist in agony as his body slumped to the ground.

Abeni's eyes opened wide as she watched Harrison, bent nearly double, sobbing on the patterned tile floor. After a long moment he looked up and lifted a trembling hand toward her. Again the lips moved but no sound came out.

"He's trying to beg her," a slight brown-skinned man shook his head sadly. "But the words just ain't coming!"

When Abeni got over the shock she could feel her anger rising. Harrison didn't say anything about all of this performance. She didn't know where else Harrison was going with it but she had some suggestions in mind as she stood up.

"Yo, girl, give him a chance," a young voice called out.

On the floor Harrison was still on his knees, still looking up at her, now with both hands open and pleading.

Abeni slid out of the booth, turned on her heel, and pushed her way through the crowd. There were some boos and catcalls and at least one woman called her a nasty name.

She barely managed to avoid a gypsy cab as she crossed Malcolm X Boulevard. She was all the way up to 138th Street before she noticed she didn't have her cell.

Back at the shop, she told Noee, "By the time I got here, I didn't need a cell, I could send out any message I had using hate waves!"

"I don't see why you went down there in the first place."

"I've been going with the man for umpteen years and he asked me for a simple favor," Abeni said. "I didn't expect him to do something stupid like screaming and hollering all over the floor in public and embarrassing me to death. People looking at me like I'm some kind of cold-hearted freak or something. They actually *booed* me like I was a baseball team or something! I wish I had taken off my shoe and beat him in his big head."

"What you crying for now?" Noee asked. "It's over, right?"

"You can say that again."

"So move on, big sister," Noee said. "Move on."

Which is exactly what Abeni Evans did for the next four months. She moved on with her work at the Curl-E-Que by taking a course in thread waxing, moved on in her personal life by starting a diary of her accomplishments, and moved her mind completely away from the entire classification known as sorry-butt Negroes.

Then Harrison called.

"Can you hear me? The traffic on Piccadilly is brutal this time of day."

"Piccadilly? Where are you?"

"I rented a little place on Jermyn Street in London," Harrison said. "Our film is being shown here and I got to tell you, it's being well received here at the Brixton festival. Two studios are thinking of picking it up for national distribution."

"What film?"

"My documentary on the war between the black man and the black woman," Boyd said. "One review said that the episode in Pam-Pam's was the strongest thing he's seen in years. I'm just wondering if you want to come over for the closing ceremonies. You're a star over here, baby. A stone star. Your picture is all over Leicester Square. I think I can get you some interviews with the BBC. What do you think?"

Abeni looked in the mirror to make sure she was awake. "Harrison Boyd, are you telling me I'm a star because I broke up with a black man?" she asked. "No, I'm not coming."

"Hey, you don't mind if I'm recording this, do you?" Harrison asked. "Matter of fact, would you mind saying the whole thing over again? Abeni? Abeni? You there?"

madonna

Looking in the mirror, I saw what I always saw, plain old me. Short hair sticking out all over my head like it ain't never seen a comb, lips too big, eyes puffy from being up all night. There ain't nothing pretty about me. I'm sixteen, and I got a baby, but that doesn't mean I'm some kind of freak. And I've never been a whore. Even though I'm up here all night wondering how I'm going to get something for Amiri. He's old enough to be eating something more than cereal, but that's all I had the money for. Money don't come knocking on your door if you poor and black.

Amiri, he's looking at me and don't even know he needs some different food. He's only nine months and is trusting in me and I ain't got nothing for him. I ain't got a job. I ain't got a daddy for him. And it don't mean nothing to him if I'm decent inside. Hungry go up against decent and it come away still hungry. So I'm sitting in the window all night looking down at 145th Street, watching the cars go by over the wet streets and the neon lights in the windows down on the avenue. Amiri didn't sleep much, either. Even when I was rocking him in my lap.

When it got light and the bodega was open I put Amiri back in his bed and got the seventy-three cents I had for more cereal. It wasn't enough for milk, I knew. I was thinking I could walk down to 125th Street to that new coffee place. They were new and still kept the milk for the coffee on the counter, and I could get some of those little containers. I knew in a few weeks they would see people taking them and then move them behind the counter with the sugar. But it was a long way to walk and to leave Amiri.

I got downstairs just as the sun was coming up over the buildings. That's when I seen Billy Carroll, John's son. Billy's about eighteen, maybe even nineteen, and classy like his father. He always treated me like people. I appreciate it when people treat me right even though I ain't got nothing going on.

"Letha, what are you doing up so early?" Billy asked. He was sitting on the stoop with his sketch pad and some square crayons or something he was drawing with.

I looked at his pad and he was drawing the buildings. Billy could draw.

"Just going to the store," I said. "What you doing up so early?"

"Wanted to get the sunrise coming over the buildings," he said. "It's close to the same effect as sunrise over the mountains, except the buildings have more red in them. When the sun hits them just right, they just about glow."

I looked at his picture and then at the buildings. He got it down right. I told him I liked his picture.

"Thanks," he said, smiling.

The rain had stopped but there were still puddles in the streets and water ran along the edge of the sidewalk toward the sewers. The neighborhood was waking up. People were coming out of their buildings going to work. A tall old man was bringing garbage cans out the side door of the supermarket. He turned them on an angle and kind of rolled them to the curb. The old black and white cat that hung around the second-hand shop was stretching itself in front of the rusty iron gates.

I went into the bodega and found the oatmeal. It was sixty-nine cents for a small box. Down near Broadway, under the el, you could get the same box for fifty-seven cents. It made me mad to have to pay twelve cents more for the cereal, but I was too tired to even think on it.

When I got back across the street Billy was still sitting on the stoop.

"Hey, Letha," he said as I started up the stairs.

"Hey, Billy," I said back.

"Letha, why don't you let me paint you?" he said. "Are you busy this morning?"

"Paint me?" I looked at him.

"I'll give you forty dollars," he said. "I'll come up to your place and do some sketches of you and take a few photos. It'll only take a couple of hours at the most. And I really need a model. These buildings get to look all the same after a while. What do you say?"

I turned and looked down at him and he was looking dead in my face. A bunch of things went through my head at the same time. The first thing was that I felt bad Billy saying that to me. Talking about coming up to my place and paying me some forty dollars. For what? I wasn't some pretty woman to be paying to have her picture painted. Was he thinking he was going to come up to my house and pay me forty dollars and do whatever he wanted to do?

It made me mad to think he was hustling me and I tried to come up with something to say back to him, something that was sharp and could cut him on down. I didn't think of nothing right away and I knew I wasn't going to think of anything. I'm not quick like that. Then I thought about having an extra forty dollars.

Forty dollars is not all the money in the world, but if your rent was already paid you could do all right on forty dollars. What you could do was buy some evaporated milk in cans and put them under the bed. Then no matter what happened Amiri would have milk. You could buy canned tuna and maybe a twenty-pound bag of rice. "When you coming up?" I asked Billy.

"About a half hour?"

"Yeah, okay," I said.

I made the cereal for Amiri. I forgot I didn't have any sugar. He didn't want the cereal but he was hungry and he ate it. He looked at me and I knew if I smiled he would smile back. That's what Amiri does. As long as I'm okay he's okay. Sometimes, when I'm alone at night and I start to cry, he'll cry, too. He knows when I'm sad, but I don't know where he got that from. It's like he was just born knowing stuff about me.

"Amiri, I don't know what Billy Carroll got in mind," I said. "I just hope it ain't no mess. He looks like he's okay, but you can't tell with men. I know you won't be mean to women when you grow up."

I said it like I was annoyed. I was, too, because I didn't think I would do just anything for money. But it was getting to be too hard. After Amiri was born I had some spotting and the doctor said I shouldn't be doing work that was "too strenuous."

"It sometimes happens with the first child," he said.

He was looking at his papers. I guessed he meant that Amiri was the first child and that I probably would have a lot more. People jump to whatever conclusions they want when you're pregnant and alone.

I looked in the mirror. I was wearing my beige blouse and a green sweater. I thought about changing, but I didn't have anything nice to change into. My blue top wasn't no improvement.

I wondered what Billy Carroll was going to say to me. What would he want for his forty dollars? Would he ask me to undress? Some of the guys in my school last year had gone around the neighborhood taking pictures of winos and junkies laid out in the street. Maybe that's what he wanted to do. Make a picture of me like I was something pitiful.

After Amiri ate I put him back on his bed and gave him the purple bunny my mother had brought over for him. I had hoped she was going to buy him some clothes, or even maybe some disposable diapers, but all she had brought was some plastic toys and that stuffed bunny. I couldn't be around her for two minutes without hearing how disappointed she was in me. Shoot, I was disappointed in myself just as much. It wasn't that I was so wonderful or anything before, but at least I went to school and didn't have any babies. Then Amiri came along.

Amiri's father was like thirty or something and I didn't

even like him. He took me to a movie and then came home with me to my mother's house. She wasn't there and he started talking about how I "owed him some loving." I knew I didn't owe that fool nothing but I did want to know what it was like to have sex. I found out. It was a sweaty man grunting and hurting me and making me feel sorry for going too far. Then it was a sweaty man saying how he had to leave to get to some business downtown. Then it was me sitting by myself, sorry for what I had done and hoping that I hadn't caught nothing or got pregnant. Then it was Amiri. Whatever I had owed his father there was no loving attached to it.

Billy knocked soft on the door. Almost like he was sneaking up on something. I didn't want to answer it, but I knew I would. He came in and I could see his eyes look around real quick.

"Sit anywhere you want," I said. There was one chair at the table and one near the bed.

"Actually, the light coming in your window is a northern light," he said. "I don't know if you understand about light, but the light that comes in from the north seems to reveal more things."

"Oh." I could see myself in the mirror over the dresser, but I wouldn't look.

"So, do you want to sit in front of the window?" he asked. He turned the chair near the bed so it faced the window, about four feet back from the sill and the same distance from the bed.

I got up and sat on the chair.

Billy sat on the edge of my bed, put his hands in his lap, and just looked at me. I had my clothes on, but I felt naked. He asked me something and I didn't catch it, and then he asked me again.

"Do you mind if I move the bed?" he asked.

I shrugged, and he moved the bed away so he could sit further away from me. Then he put his hands in his lap again and just looked at me.

Then, after a long time, he picked up his drawing pad. I could hear the scratching on the paper. He was drawing me.

I wondered if he was going to draw me and then tell me to take my clothes off. He hadn't said anything about messing with me yet. He hadn't said anything about the forty dollars, either. There was no way I was going to feel good. People looking at me like that made me feel bad and he should have known it. Maybe he did but just didn't care. I tried to roll my eyes over to one side and see myself in the mirror again. All the while he was drawing.

The room was filled with the sound of Billy's drawing and the even sound of Amiri's breathing. I knew my son was asleep. There was a clock on the refrigerator, but I couldn't see it or hear its ticking. My stomach began to cramp and I felt bad.

All Billy was doing was drawing me, like he said he would. And where I was feeling bad before about needing the money, almost bad enough to let him mess with me if he had wanted, now I felt ugly and he was writing down just how ugly I was.

"How about some photographs?" Billy asked.

He took a lot of photographs. He asked me to hold Amiri and he took some with both of us in the picture.

"What do you think of your son?" he asked me.

"I love him to death," I said. "What do you think?"

"Hold him like you love him," he said.

He took more photographs and I asked him to take one of just Amiri so I could send it to his grandmother. He said okay, but I could see he was more interested in taking pictures of me holding Amiri.

Billy gave me the money like he said he would. He said he was going to move the bed back but I said, "Let me feel how it's like over there for a while."

"Okay," he said, smiling. "I'll try to finish the picture sometime this week, maybe by the first part of next week."

He wrapped all of his stuff up, making sure that I didn't see any of his drawings.

When Billy left, with his stuff under his arm, I didn't even know how to feel. I just sat there in the room for a while, trying to think of what had happened. I looked in the mirror again, and saw that I still looked a mess.

I went to the window and started thinking about the forty dollars, what I would buy with it. I wanted to run right down to the store, but I didn't want Billy to see me just then. When I looked at the clock on the dresser it was past noon. Amiri wasn't crying but he would be, soon. The boy knows how to eat.

In the supermarket I thought about Billy's picture and wished I had at least combed my hair. Then I remembered the blue blouse I had worn to my mother's house two Sundays ago, the one with the lace around the top. I should have worn that.

The cart was half filled when I saw this dude standing across from me. He was looking at me and I tried to ignore him, but then he followed me down the next aisle and stopped when I stopped.

"What you looking at me for?" I asked him. Amiri was on my hip.

"I hope you got the money to pay for that stuff," he said.

"Get out my face, creep!" That's what I said.

He was looking at me like I was a thief or something. He got a mean look on his face and crossed his arms. I was hungry and Amiri was starting to whimper and he would be crying soon. I put a pack of diapers in the cart and pushed it to the checkout. What I bought came to twenty-one dollars and three cents. I paid for it, gave the jerk who followed me a look, and started home.

Billy was on my mind all week, mostly because of the money he gave me. Amiri and I had enough to carry us through until there was more money in my welfare account. I don't daydream about men usually, but I dreamed about him. I'm nothing special and men usually just want to get in between my legs and get on their way. So when he didn't hit on me it made me feel good. To Billy I was something else he could draw, like the sun coming up or a car or a tree. I liked that, being ordinary. I also wondered what I would say if he did hit on me. Probably yes, but I didn't think about that too much.

Almost two weeks had passed when Billy knocked on my door one morning. I saw he had the case he carried his stuff in. I was looking a little tacky, but the place wasn't too tore up so I asked him if he wanted to come in.

"I've got the portrait," he said. "I finished it from the photographs. Can I show it to you?"

"Sure." I could see he was happy with it. He unzipped his case near the window and I sat down on the chair. Amiri pulled himself up on the side of his crib and made some noises like he was trying to talk.

"Well, there it is," Billy said, propping the picture on the dresser. "What do you think?"

The boy could really paint. I liked the picture a lot, especially the way he painted Amiri. Because it looked just like him. It was mostly blue mixed with gray except for the girl and Amiri, who were brown but a nice brown that went with the blue in a way and stood out from it, too.

"It's real good," I said, looking closer. "That is just like Amiri. You painted him but it could be a photograph."

"And your portrait?" he asked.

"That's not me," I said. "It kind of favors my face shape, but that's not me."

"It's you," he said. "It's the best portrait I've ever done. It's exactly how I see you. I call it *Madonna and Child*."

I looked again. The girl in the picture did favor me, but she was really pretty. There was something nice about her, like she was good people. And I really liked the way she was holding Amiri. I remembered how Billy had told me to hold Amiri like I loved him. And the way the girl was holding him was just like that.

"I'm going to enter this picture in a group show in Brooklyn that's opening next week," Billy said. "But I'd like you to have it for a while. Let me know what you think about it after a few days."

"Okay," I said.

Billy asked me to be careful with the picture and I said I would. For some reason I couldn't wait until he left. When he did I looked at the picture really close. Then I looked at myself in the mirror. It was funny because all my parts were there, my eyes, my mouth, my right ear, and my nose. But there was something else in the picture, almost like Billy had seen something that I couldn't see. I tried to fix my face like the me he had painted, but it was still different.

Amiri wanted to touch the picture but I didn't let him. He looked at it and made his baby noises and I knew he recognized us. I held him in front of it the way Billy had painted us. Every time I did I had to kiss Amiri, that's the way the picture made me feel.

By the end of the second day I couldn't take my eyes off Billy's painting. I thought I was going to look all the paint off of it. So when I saw Billy on the street and he said he was coming to pick it up I wasn't so happy.

"I'll take you out to the show when it opens," he said.

I didn't go. For some reason I was just happy to have seen the picture in my room. Billy said somebody was thinking about buying it but he wasn't sure about selling it because he liked it so much. I didn't really care if he sold it because, in a way, I was always going to have that picture somewhere in my head. That and the memory of how Billy looked that day, how serious he was working on his drawings. Sometimes I try to imagine what he was thinking when he was in my little apartment and it makes me feel good. It does.

It's been months since I had Billy's painting in my house. Sometimes, when things get bad for me and Amiri, I pick him up and stand in front of the mirror and I can see just how we looked in Billy's picture. When I look in the mirror I can see just how much I love Amiri, the same way that Billy saw it. Knowing that Billy, that someone can look inside of you and see something good is worth more than the forty dollars he gave me. It is.

the
real
deal

John Carroll was not in a good mood. He hated to see young black couples having difficulties with the mysteries of love. In his innermost heart he truly believed in the power of love to save the community and uplift the race. The fact that he had been part of bringing trouble to Mavis and Calvin bothered him, but there wasn't a lot he could do about it because Calvin was, after all, a fully grown man. A young man, perhaps, but a man.

It had all started the day that Sister Inez Tubbs was sitting at the table near the window complaining that his curried crab cakes didn't have enough curry in them. The arthritis in his right ankle was bothering him something terrible, and then Mavis Brown had come busting into his shop with Calvin Williams asking about where he could get a part-time job to buy a gun.

"Boy, what you need a gun for?" John had asked, putting down the rag he was using to wipe off his counter.

"He needs a gun because he's got to deal with Leon," Mavis said. "Leon has been running his mouth up and down the avenue talking about *how* I ain't this and *how* I ain't that and *how* I was trying to be with him and he didn't want me."

"Calvin, a lot of couples break up and leave a trail of bitter feelings," John Carroll said. "Why don't you just go over and talk to Leon? I'm sure you can settle it without getting into violence."

"No, man, it ain't like that," Calvin said. "He knows I'm going out with Mavis so if he's talking trash it means he's trying to punk me out. He thinks I'm like I used to be—you know, all talk and no action. I'm eighteen now and I got to let the real me out."

"And who's the real you?" John Carroll asked.

"I'm hard, man," Calvin said. "People look at me and think I'm soft because I let things slide. But as far as I'm concerned the slide part is done and the new ride has begun."

"And he wants to clear up all his loose ends so he can concentrate on his new rap album," Mavis added.

"Oh, I got you." John Carroll sat down at the counter. "You going to be a rapper and you getting hard now."

"I've always been hard," Calvin said.

"Well, why don't you come around about twelve this afternoon?" John Carroll said. "I need to make a little trip upstate and I could use somebody to keep me company. You come on with me and I'll give you some money toward your gun and introduce you to somebody who can tell you where to get it."

"John Carroll!" Sister Tubbs tightened her mouth up so she looked like a frog with a toothache.

"Inez, you are sixty-five years old," John Carroll said. "Isn't that kind of late in life to be growing another nose? I know you can't have but one nose the way you keep nosing into my business."

"You're supposed to be a leader on this block and you helping this boy get a gun!" Sister Tubbs stood up, gave John Carroll a dirty look, and stormed out of the roti shop.

"Be here at twelve-thirty, Calvin," John Carroll said. "I'm afraid you can't come, Mavis."

"It's man business, baby," Calvin said.

John Carroll watched as Calvin and Mavis left, then got his son, Billy, on the phone and asked him to come look after the shop.

"I got to go see some old friends upstate," John said. "You're not busy, are you?"

Billy said he would come, although John knew he didn't want to work in the hot store on a summer afternoon.

Calvin came back on time and showed John Carroll the twenty-eight dollars he had to buy the gun.

"How much you think I need to buy a nine?" he asked as they settled into John Carroll's Escalade.

"A decent nine-millimeter should cost about one-eighty," John Carroll said. "But you can probably pick up something on the street for seventy or eighty used."

"Well, I got to do what I got to do," Calvin said.

The drive from Harlem to Stormville, New York, took two hours and ten minutes with a short stop for gas on the way. John Carroll asked Calvin about his new rap album as the station attendant wiped his windshield.

"What I want to do is to bring truth to the people," Calvin said. "A lot of guys out here rapping and it's all about bling-bling and it don't really mean a thing because everybody can't be into that bling-bling thing. You know what I mean?"

"Yes, I do," John Carroll said. "That's what I was telling my friend when I called after you left this morning. I could tell you weren't into anything fake or halfway. You wanted the real deal."

"Yeah, people got to know where you coming from so they can know if you just blowing air or you on the square," Calvin said. "This guy we meeting, he's a down dude?"

"Yeah!" John Carroll glanced over at Calvin. "You know I'm for real, don't you?"

"Yeah, man, you're people."

"And you know I didn't always run no roti shop?"

"I didn't know that," Calvin said. "What did you do before that?"

"Prison, brother."

"You were in prison?"

"Assistant warden," John Carroll said. "Retired ten years ago and opened the shop. I know all the big-time gangsters, guys who really keep it real. That's why I set up a meeting between you and Bubba Jones."

"He's an assistant warden, too?"

"No, man." John Carroll stopped at the perimeter gate and shook hands with the guard who came over. The square-shouldered man directed him toward one of the parking lots and John moved the car smoothly past the small building and the rotating cameras. "Bubba is a prisoner and the hardest man you ever want to meet. He knows everything that happens on the street. He used to live right down from the armory. You know where they closed that repair shop and rehabbed that building? Put them green awnings out?"

"Yeah." Calvin nodded.

The waiting room of Greenhaven Correctional Facility was filled with visitors, many of them young women with small children. Most of them black or Spanish.

"You don't have any guns or knives on you now, do you?" John Carroll whispered.

Calvin shook his head. "Man, this is tough," he said. "I could rap about this big-time. You know, rhyme about doing time. You know, if you going to wear the poet crown you can slow it down if you got the time to serve even if you didn't deserve the rap. Yo, Mr. John Carroll, I'm feeling it, man. No lie."

"I thought you might," John Carroll said.

John Carroll went through the security search first, taking off his shoes so the guards could put them through the X-ray machine, then going through the metal detector. Calvin followed and John Carroll watched as the guards searched him and then stamped his hand with the indelible ink.

"Why they do that?" Calvin asked as they went into the elevator.

"So they can check you when you leave," John Carroll said. "You don't have that ink mark, you're not leaving."

The Section 3 Visitors Room had a large eight-sided table and John Carroll and Calvin found seats and talked while they waited for the inmates to be let in. John Carroll asked Calvin if he really loved Mavis.

"I don't know if I love her," Calvin said. "But I go for her. You know, she's got it going on, but she was going with that other dude for so long I think she still might have some feeling for him. I got to check that out before I get too far into her."

"Yeah, women are funny that way," John Carroll said. "Hey, here comes Bubba now."

Bubba Jones was six foot five inches tall. Big, bald-headed, and black. He grinned when he saw John Carroll and came over.

"Hey, Captain," he said. He reached across the table and shook John Carroll's hand.

"How you doing, Bubba?"

"I'm good, man," Bubba said. "You know I don't have no visitors since my aunt died, but I'm getting by. How you doing? You looking good."

"Feeling good, too," John Carroll said. "Got a little arthritis here and there, but it ain't no big thing. Did they tell you I was going to tighten up your commissary thing?"

"Yeah, and you know I appreciate it," Bubba said. "Only thing that makes the day go by in here is buying a few things once in a while. Hey, did you know that Wright got out? Guy that robbed the bank down on Forty-second Street?"

"They paroled him?" John Carroll asked.

"They paroled him just before Christmas and that fool was back here two weeks after New Year's," Bubba said.

The room had filled with other inmates and was getting a little noisy. John Carroll told Calvin, "Move a little closer. You don't want to be shouting your business out in here. Bubba, this is Calvin, the young man I called you about."

Bubba reached across the table and wrapped his huge hand around Calvin's.

"How do you do?"

"I'm doing okay," Bubba said. "You a youngblood, right?"

"No, I'm eighteen," Calvin said.

"Bubba, Calvin's got the same problem you had," John Carroll said. "People dissing him."

"That's what happened to you?" Calvin asked.

"Yeah, man. Sucker dissed me right there on Malcolm X Boulevard between a Hundred and Forty-fifth and a Hundred and Forty-sixth Street. Called me a low-lifed, stink breath moron and then had the nerve to pull a gun on me!"

"Then what happened?"

"I stabbed him in the eye with the ice pick I was carrying," Bubba said. "When I done that he kind of doubled over and his right leg started twitching and jumping and he was moaning and turning in a circle. Man, it was a funny thing to see. I snatched the gun out his hand and stabbed him again, and he was kind of staggering up and down the street, and the way he was jerking around was really something to see. I ain't *never* seen anything like that but once since then. That was when they killed that boy here in the shower."

"They killed somebody here in the prison?"

"Somebody's always being killed or cut up in here," John Carroll said.

"It ain't no big thing," Bubba said. "You get used to it. It's like when winter comes—you wear a big coat. When summer comes, you take it off. In here, you watch your back. That's the way it goes. But you don't see no cutting or stabbing during the checker tournaments. People got their minds on the tournament and that keeps things cool."

"Didn't this guy play in the tournaments?" John Carroll nodded toward a tall pale-looking man.

Bubba turned, saw the man, and sucked his teeth.

"Chiba? That fool can't play no checkers," he said. "You know he went and filed a complaint about his sentence because he's not eligible for parole. His family paid for the appeal, too."

"Everybody wants to get out, Bubba," John Carroll said.

"How he going to get out when he done killed a whole family and their dog?" Bubba asked. "And I owe him two packs of cigarettes. I bet the Knicks was going to make the playoffs."

"You can pay him with the money I left for you in the commissary," John Carroll said.

"Yeah, well . . ." Bubba hesitated. "Look, Captain, you mind if I do a little business right quick?"

"No, go on," John Carroll said.

"Yo, Chiba!" Bubba called, and waved the other man over.

The man looked at John Carroll, recognized him, and then looked at Calvin.

"Yo, Chiba!" Bubba called to him again. "Come here, man."

Chiba Banks was just under six feet tall, with brown skin, cold gray eyes, and lips that twisted in a frozen sneer. He came over and sat on the inmates' side of the table, his eyes fixed on John Carroll.

"I thought you was dead," he rasped.

"I'm still here," John Carroll said.

"Hey, what's your name again?" Bubba leaned forward excitedly as he spoke to Calvin.

"Calvin Williams."

"Calvin, my man, just stand up once and turn around," Bubba said. "All the way around."

"Why?" Calvin asked.

"A favor for me," Bubba said. "No big thing. You can do a favor for a brother in the slam, right? We all in the struggle together and everything. You know what I mean?"

Calvin looked at John Carroll, then stood and turned around and sat back down.

"Look, Chiba, I'll trade you Malvin or Calvin here for them two packs of cigarettes I owe you," Bubba said. "He's only eighteen, man."

"What I look like to you, something stupid?" Chiba's voice sounded like sandpaper on glass. "He ain't in here, he's still in the world."

"Yo, but he's getting a gun—Captain told me." Bubba

lowered his voice. "They catch him with a nine he got five years. And he live on a Hundred and Forty-fifth Street in Harlem, so this would be where they send him."

"Not if he just rob somebody," Chiba said, covering his mouth with his hand. "You got to kill somebody to get up here or use the gun during a felony."

"You can just shoot a sucker and get to Greenhaven! He don't have to die," Bubba said. "Ain't that right, Captain?"

"It depends on what space they got and if the judge thinks you're violent or not," John Carroll said.

"He's eighteen and he wants a gun, you know he's violent!" Bubba said. "And he's pretty. You seen him turn around."

"Hey, I don't go with no men," Calvin said. "I'm too hard for that crap."

"Ain't that how you like them, Chiba?" Bubba put his hand on Chiba's arm and Chiba snatched it away. "You like them when they got some fight in them!"

"Hey, I ain't even about no prison!" Calvin said.

"Shut up and sit down, pussy!" Chiba said.

Calvin looked at John Carroll and John Carroll looked the other way, toward the dirty, barred windows.

"Okay, I'll let you slide on the cigarettes for a year." Chiba's mouth barely moved as he talked to Bubba. "But if he ain't in the system within a year you still owe me one pack. Deal or no deal?"

"Deal!" Bubba answered.

Chiba looked around the room. "You can slide with both packs if he gives me a kiss right now."

"And so when you asked him about the gun what did he say?" Abeni asked Mavis as she trimmed the hair from her neck into a neat V.

"He had the nerve to tell me to shut up and get out his face," Mavis said.

"Girl, you got to stop wiggling your neck if you want me to cut it straight!"

"Here he was loving me at noon and then at five-fifteen he was looking at me like I had bad breath or something, and talking about how he had a *true reflection* to go in a *new direction*," Mavis said. "What I think is either John Carroll told that boy some lies about me or the heat is getting to his dumb butt."

"Mavis, when I was thirteen my father told me something." Abeni put down the clippers. "He said never to worry about getting a boyfriend. He said there are as many of them as there are leaves on a tree. When the time comes they're coming down to see you. And if you don't see what you want there's going to be a whole new crop the next year."

"I know that, Abeni," Mavis said. "But when Leon put me down one week and then Calvin shows up lame the next, I'm beginning to think something's wrong with me."

"Mavis, look at yourself in the mirror, girl." Abeni turned the chair so Mavis could see herself full-face. "Are you fine or what?"

Mavis looked at herself in the mirror, then turned her head slightly to one side, and had to smile.

"Yes, I am fine."

"I told you," Abeni said. "Sometimes the brothers just can't deal."

marisol
and
skeeter

I'm not the kind of girl who goes around getting into other people's business and I definitely don't want you in mine. Also, don't be jumping up in my face because I don't like that, either. So when this snap-happy chick at the pool hall starts running her mouth about the way I dress and had the nerve, when I had politely asked her to shut her stupid mouth, to step in front of me and shake her fake fingernails in my face—well, I naturally went upside her head. Several times. With a pool cue. That is how I ended up watching television at Sunrise House on Christmas Eve. I had done twenty days of a sixty-day deck and I had eight more to serve at Sunrise, which is a residency joint for girls on their way out of the joint. It was Christmas Eve and the word came down that anybody who had a place to go to could split. The thing was that my mother went to the Dominican Republic the week before and I had left my keys with her, so I didn't have anyplace to go. I was seventeen and knew my way around, but I still didn't have anywhere to crash, so there I was holding down the place by myself. Only other people there was an old security dude and this Jewish lady, Mrs. Goldklank, who works at the place. She sent out for some sandwiches and we ate them and watched television most of the day. It was wack, but I felt so down I didn't even have the energy to get up off the couch.

The city had hired a band for entertainment and Mrs. Goldklank thought they had canceled it when everybody else went home. But around nine o'clock a little band showed up. They called themselves the All Star Stompers. They had already been paid for the job and when they found out everybody was gone they didn't know what to do. Mrs. Goldklank said they might as well leave.

"How come you here?" the leader of the band asked. He was about my age, eighteen, brown-skinned, nothing special except he had nice eyes.

"I'm just here," I said. "No big thing."

"Well, I guess I'll play for you."

The other players, three black dudes and a white chick, gave him a look.

"Hey, y'all can go," he said. "Merry Christmas!"

Then he took out his saxophone and started playing Christmas carols.

I wasn't in the mood for no Christmas carols so I just sat on a chair and watched television. He kept on playing.

"What you playing for?" I asked him.

"Because it's Christmas Eve and I'm Skeeter Bramwell and I want you to be happy on Christmas Eve," he said. "So I'm going to keep on playing until you give me a genuine smile. Then I can pack up and go home."

He smiled and I kind of smiled back at him and he kept playing. He was good, and it was funny having a guy sit real close to you and play just for you. I finally broke down and gave him a smile.

"Thank you for playing for me."

"How long you got to stay in here?"

"I could go now if I had a place of my own."

He gave me a long look, then pulled out his business card and twenty dollars and handed them to me.

"I don't want your money!" I said, handing back the money and the card.

He looked hurt, he really did. I realized he didn't mean anything bad, so I took the card back. Not the money, though.

"I don't know what your name is," he said, "but I hope you're going to be okay. And if you ever get around my way, and you see me on the street, give me another one of those nice smiles of yours."

"My name is Marisol," I said. "Marisol Vegas. And I'll save a special smile for you."

Then he left and for some reason I was liking him. Maybe it was his eyes, or the way he played for me. I don't know, but he seemed okay.

When I got out I knew I had to get my life together. I had met some hard women in the joint and from what I heard they spent half their lives coming in and out. Still, I didn't know what to do. I found a little piece of job on 135th Street, down the street from the YMCA. I was selling glazed donuts—sprinkles or no sprinkles, you had a choice—and Skeeter came in. He recognized me and smiled.

We talked a little and he asked me if I wanted to go out for coffee after work. I was thinking *not really* after working all day in a coffee shop, but I said yes and that's how we started getting to know each other.

Skeeter Bramwell worked here and there, like half the guys in the world, but what he loved most was playing sax. He told me his father had put the All Star Stompers together. I asked him if it was supposed to be a jazz band.

"It depends on who's playing," he said. "Mostly I just round up whoever wants to play and we go out on any gigs we can find."

"Your father brought you into the business?"

"Naw," Skeeter said. "He didn't have much time for me. Didn't have much time for my moms, either, if you know what I mean. I learned to play on my own, and when I heard he died I went and asked if I could try out for the band. They said I could have it if I wanted it."

The way I figured, Skeeter was sort of thrown away, like me. His mother raised him and I guess she did the best she could, but from the way he talked she was running the streets a lot, too.

We started hanging out steady. What I liked about Skeeter was that when you talked to him you got the feeling he was really listening, really wanted to hear what you were saying. Most guys I know will just uh-huh you to death while they're scheming on how to get you into bed. Skeeter didn't even hit on me right away. Sometimes we would just go and sit in St. Nicholas Park and watch the children play—he liked children. Or we would go to a movie. When his band got a gig I would go and hear them play. I don't know the exact day I got serious about him. I wasn't even sure that I was serious, but I took him over to my aunt Nilda's house and afterward she told me I was in love.

"Why don't you find a boy from the Dominican Republic?" she asked. "Somebody with good hair?"

Before Aunt Nilda ran her mouth I wasn't even thinking about being in love, but once she let it out I realized that maybe I did love him. We started messing around now and then and making plans about what we were going to do and Skeeter had some nice ideas of what he wanted from life, including having a family.

"But if I have a family," he said, "I got to be there with them. I can't be running around dipping here and dipping there like my old man. I want something serious."

I believed in Skeeter when he said that. I felt like I could look into his heart and see that he was telling the truth. He had a room downtown, a kitchenette, and I fixed it up for him. I got two pairs of drapes from the Goodwill Center and put one pair at his window and sewed the other pair together to make a bedspread. I got him some nice plates and we bought a mirror and hung it over his dresser, which made the room look bigger. We were getting real close and I was about as happy as I had ever remembered. Then I got pregnant.

My mother was all upset and deep into nine kinds of drama and explaining to me how my life was going steady downhill. I felt bad telling Aunt Nilda but she showed big-time and helped me get a kitchenette in her building.

To me, getting pregnant was scary, but it wasn't the end of the world. I loved Skeeter and he said he loved me. I had seen a lot of girls get pregnant and end up as just another baby mama with the guy coming around whenever he felt like it and arguing all the time. I didn't expect that from Skeeter. But I didn't expect him to get all depressed, either.

Skeeter wanted to be a good father, and I knew he did, but he couldn't find a good job and I could see where that was messing with him.

"I need . . . I got to have a place for us that's a real home," he said.

What I was hoping for was for Skeeter just to change his mind or to get lucky and find a job maybe with the city or with a department store. What he was doing was working with the band at night and selling hats and gloves down on Twenty-second Street during the day. None of that made any money except when it rained and he sold umbrellas down near Penn Station. On the other hand, I was wondering whether Skeeter was just using not having a good place to stay as an excuse. What I wanted was a real good job to show up, or for Skeeter or me to hit the lottery so that when we got the money I could find out once and for all what was happening. I believed in Skeeter, and I loved him, but I just couldn't wait forever.

"Maybe you could go back to school and get a degree in something," I said.

"Or at least my GED," Skeeter said. "A real college degree is going to take years. Now, if I had me some turntables I could make some good money as a DJ. But I ain't got the money to get the turntables to make the money."

"How much do they cost?" I asked.

"You can pick up a good set downtown for about six hundred dollars if you got credit," Skeeter said. "Earl has a real nice set—tables, mixer, and everything—he wants six Benjamins for."

Okay, I knew Earl had a shop on 145th Street and he was a straight-up guy. But Earl didn't give credit, so we needed to come up with the whole six hundred. I didn't have any idea where we were going to get that much money. But sometimes cool things happen to me—that's because I live right—and when I was getting my hair done I heard that guy from the roti shop telling Mama Evans about how when he was a kid they used to have rent parties to raise money, so I asked him about it. His name was John Carroll.

"When I was coming up, if your money ran out before the month did," Mr. Carroll said, "some people would give a party and charge a quarter or fifty cents at the door to get in. They'd sell food and cut the card games and make enough money to pay the rent and have a good time doing it."

"You didn't have to pay the rent," I said. "You could do anything you wanted with the money, right?"

"Yeah, I guess so," Mr. Carroll said. "But for us it was the rent that we needed."

I couldn't wait to tell Skeeter about my idea. When I got him on the phone he was down on Forty-sixth Street buying new reeds for his horn. He wasn't as enthusiastic as I was.

"How we going to have a rent party when we don't have a place?" he asked. "My room is so small we'd have to bring in one couple at a time to dance."

"We could just have it in one of the backyards," I said.

I don't know where that came from or exactly where it was going, but I was getting desperate. The thing was, I was beginning to dream big about what me and Skeeter were going to do and I just didn't want to let that go. Not that easy, anyway. I was three and a half months pregnant and I knew I was going to be showing so I needed to get us going.

"You got to tell me how that works," he said. "You want to meet me this afternoon and we can talk about it?"

"Not this afternoon, baby," I said. "I have to go to the clinic. I'll call you tonight."

"Yeah, okay."

"Mama Evans, you ever hear of a rent party in a backyard if you don't have any other place to hold it in?"

Mama Evans was putting out new magazines on the tables in the waiting area. "No, I haven't, Marisol, but that doesn't mean it can't be done. I guess one day one of the Wright brothers walked up to somebody and asked if they had ever heard of an airplane. Just because it's new don't mean it's wrong, girl."

"That's what I always say, Mama Evans."

"Of course it's going to be hard to keep people from sneaking into your party."

That was going to be a problem. Some people would probably sneak in but most people are all right and would pay a dollar or two, I thought. And the more I thought about it the more I knew I believed in Skeeter. Skeeter had made me feel so good up in Sunrise House, I knew he could make people feel good at the party, too. That's what I told Earl over at his shop.

"And you could even put a sign out saying something about shopping at Earl's for good used furniture and antiques," I said.

"I've never heard of a rent party to buy turntables," Earl said, scratching the stubble on his chin.

"Earl, if the Wright brothers came up to you and asked you if you had ever heard of an airplane, what would you say?" I asked.

"I know what an airplane is now," he said, smiling.

"So now you know what our rent party is all about," I said. "Isn't that cool?"

"And you want me to lend Skeeter the turntables so he can make enough money to buy them?"

"I knew you would get it right away!"

"Yeah, well, all right," he said. "It can't do any harm. I guess."

The party was my idea. The idea of having it in the backyard behind John Carroll's roti shop was his. He sold food in the shop and also set up a grill in the yard. Everything else was all Skeeter.

Skeeter set up the turntables and started playing a little after seven. People who hadn't seen the flyers we put around the hood heard the music and wondered where it came from. I sat in the back of the roti shop, where they had this huge kitchen with four ovens, and collected the money. It was hot in the kitchen and I drank so many sodas I had to pee a hundred times before the night was out, but it was okay because I was so happy.

Skeeter knew every song out there and everybody was happy with the way he kept things going. He would call out a number and say, "This is for the young people in love who need to be holding each other close," and all the young people would get up and dance. Then he would play something for the old people who needed to get their shake-shake-shake on.

"And if you don't know what a shake-shake-shake is don't worry about it," he said. "Just get out on the floor and wiggle your parts until you figure it out."

I almost strained my neck trying to see what the people were doing. Everyone was having a good time and

John Carroll said business was so good he might have to have two or three parties every month.

We made four hundred and nine dollars on the door. Skeeter put some money with it and got the turntables from Earl.

"Baby, we got the turntables and sixty-nine dollars toward our place," Skeeter said. We had brought the tables to my house and were sitting on the sofa with me leaning against him and his arm around me. "I think we're on our way."

Skeeter gave me the sixty-nine dollars and told me to do anything with it I wanted to. I knew he thought I was just going to save it but I thought I should buy him something nice with it to show him that I was really feeling what he was doing. So after I went up to the clinic and had my first sonogram I went down to the new store on 125th Street.

The store had three floors and it was just supposed to be smoking. When it opened the mayor was there and the ceremony was in all the papers. But when I showed up it was dead. There were some clerks standing around trying to act cute and a lady in a cleaning outfit watching one of those televisions they had put up in a corner. Other than that they had more security guards than customers.

I looked around for a sweater because I thought Skeeter would look good in a pullover. I found some but they were going for over a hundred each so I just kept walking.

"May I help you?"

I turned and saw this tall guy wearing a suit and a carnation so I figured he must be the manager or something. "How come you don't have any people in here?" I asked.

"Well, it's a relatively new store," he said. He was looking around the whole time he was talking to me like he had something else to do. "It takes time for people to understand what better merchandise is all about."

"Are you hiring any new people?" I asked.

"Not at the moment," he said, pulling out a handkerchief and wiping at his face. "You can leave an application in the third-floor office if you'd like."

"Who's the—" He had already started away. "Yo, don't walk away from me when I'm talking to you!"

He stopped, turned his big head, and looked me up and down like I was dirty or something. Then he came back over to me and asked me what else I wanted.

"Two things. First, I want to know where I can find the manager of this store," I said.

"Third floor," he said, looking down his nose. "Ask for Mr. Reuben. And the other thing was?"

"I just want you to know that you should try to join the human race. They're taking anything now."

He turned on one heel and walked away shaking his

head. The truth was that I would not have cut him under any circumstances because that's not the kind of girl I am. But as stuck-up as that fool was I could tell that he *needed* cutting and it probably wouldn't be too long before somebody did it for him. In the meanwhile I had better things to do.

I told Skeeter I'd be at his house when he got home and I was. I had brought a quart of pepper steak, a quart of shrimp fried rice, and an order of butterfly shrimp.

"Girl, you up to something," Skeeter said when he saw the food. "You don't even like shrimp."

Skeeter only had a little card table with folding legs but I had bought a tablecloth from Job Lot and a white vase with flowers painted on it so it looked nice. I put the plates out and some food while he watched me. I didn't want to smile or anything, but I knew he was watching and I did smile a little. Also, he knew I had something on my mind. We were getting close like that, with him knowing little things about me and me knowing little things about him, like how he was going to say "no way" when I told him my idea.

"So guess where I was this afternoon?" I said.

"You told me you were going to the clinic," he said. "How did everything turn out there?"

"It turned out good," I said. "And I felt good so I walked down to a Hundred and Twenty-fifth Street, to that big store on the corner. You know which one I mean? They had all the mannequins dressed in those striped shirts that time?"

"Right down from the Magic Johnson theater."

"The manager, Mr. Reuben, seemed okay," I said. "Kind of downtown white. He was wearing his suit inside his office like he thought some television cameras were going to show up or something."

"Mr. who?"

"Mr. Reuben," I said. "He's the one who wants to talk to you."

"Talk to me about what?" Skeeter had his head back and turned to one side.

"About you setting up a DJ booth in the store," I said. I finished with the table. "I didn't get any wonton soup because it didn't look too fresh."

"What does this guy know about me and about me being a DJ?" Skeeter said.

So I told him about the guy walking around with the carnation in his lapel looking at me like he was somebody. I told him about me finding the office and asking to speak to Mr. Reuben. I didn't tell him that I refused to leave until Mr. Reuben came out of his office, but I let him know that I told Mr. Reuben that his store was empty because it was like an undertaking parlor, and that he should have some music and at least talk to Skeeter.

"That he should talk to me?"

"And I said you can set up a DJ studio right in his store and young people would come in and listen to you and think it was a jumping place. We made an appointment with his executive board for Thursday morning at nine-thirty."

"No, that ain't happening," Skeeter said. "No way. I can work a party but I don't know nothing about working no department store—and I don't even have a suit so there's no way I'm going to a board meeting Thursday."

I just sat there at the table with my hands folded in front of me.

"Marisol, honey, I love you and I'm really going to try hard to make a home for us," Skeeter said. He lifted my hands from my lap and held them in his. "But I'm just Skeeter, baby. Maybe, one day, you know, I'll get a whole lot of stuff together and be more than I am now, but right now, I'm just plain old Skeeter."

He did love me and I felt it whenever I was around him. He put his forehead down on his hands, which were still holding mine, and he looked so miserable.

"Would you meet with him just to see how it turns out?"

"Baby, I'm not ready yet," he said. "You have to understand that."

"I do," I said. "It's just that . . . I told Dulce that you were going to try. For her. I know she doesn't understand, either, but maybe she can feel it."

"Who?"

"I had the sonogram today," I said. I was crying a little but I got up a smile to go along with it. "The doctor said I was going to have a little girl. And I was thinking that we would name her together, but until we picked out a permanent name I'd call her by the name they used to call my grandmother—Dulce. It means sweet. Is that okay with you?"

"You going to have a girl? You saw one of them pictures of her?"

"Yeah. And I told her you were going to go see Mr. Reuben even though you might not get the job."

"How you going to tell her that when she can't understand anything yet?"

"She knows how you feel about her, right?" I said. "And I know you would do anything for her, right?"

All day Wednesday at the donut shop I kept my cell phone off because I didn't want Skeeter calling me up and saying that he had changed his mind about going to see Mr. Reuben. I knew Mr. Reuben could make him look bad, ask him a whole bunch of questions about where he had worked and where he had went to school, that kind of thing. I felt a little scared for him but if Skeeter got a steady job right in Harlem everything would work out just perfect. I had seen an apartment on 116th Street near the 3 train. It wasn't anything fancy but I thought we could pull it off. We could have one bedroom like a studio for Skeeter to practice in for the first year and then, when Dulce got about sixteen months, we could buy a daybed and that would be her bedroom. At first I thought I would put wallpaper in the living room, then I changed my mind and then I changed it back again because I have always wanted an apartment with wallpaper somewhere in it.

Thursday morning I met Skeeter at the employees' entrance of the store and we went in. We looked good. The security guard looked over his list, found our names, and sent us up to the third floor.

The table we sat at was so big it couldn't even have fit in Skeeter's apartment.

"So, your wife tells me that you have a plan to increase the store's business." Mr. Reuben sat at the head of the table. There was a woman on one side and two men on the other. One of them was Mr. Carnation. "Tell us about it."

"I can show you," Skeeter said. "I can get some music going and people will come in and listen to it. People like music."

"We don't need dancers," Carnation said. "We need people who buy clothing."

"That's true, that's true," Skeeter said. "But first you need people to walk into the store. Then maybe you have a chance of selling them something. They'll come and listen and look around and see all the nice stuff you got."

"What kind of music would you play?" the woman asked.

"In the morning I could play some old-school stuff," Skeeter said. "Mellow, maybe even a little doo-wop. Then in the afternoon, when school lets out, I could swing into some reggae and a little soul with a touch of hip-hop."

"Doesn't sound like much of a marketing plan," Carnation said.

"Doo-wop?" Mr. Reuben said. "You remember Little Anthony and the Imperials?"

" 'Tears on My Pillow'!" Skeeter said.

"Yeah, yeah." Mr. Reuben got a faraway look in his eyes like he was remembering something good. "What was that other thing they did? Shimmy something?"

" 'Shimmy, Shimmy, Ko Ko Bop'!" Skeeter said.

Right then and there it was a done deal! The next thing we knew we were talking about how much money Skeeter expected. Me and Skeeter had agreed to ask for five hundred dollars a week if it got to talking about money, but when Mr. Reuben asked about doo-wop and Skeeter knew what he was talking about I spoke up and said we could do it for seven hundred a week. It just came out of my mouth.

"Well, that's a little steep," Mr. Reuben said. "How about . . . five hundred and twenty-five dollars?"

Outside Skeeter got weak in his legs and had to lean

against the wall for a while before we went to the sub-way. I told him to tell Dulce that he had got the job. He looked at me and just smiled.

The next Monday morning he set up on the second floor, across from the shoe department, and started steady-pumping music to the world.

In a few weeks they put in a little music department and put Skeeter inside it and pretty soon the whole joint was jumping, especially after school. And Skeeter was so happy he was smiling all the time.

We had our wedding a month later on 125th Street and St. Nicholas at St. Joseph's. I wore a white satin dress I bought and my aunt Nilda made me a lace top that looked perfect with it. Skeeter's old group, the All Star Stompers, played and my mother didn't bad-mouth any-body during the whole party, which was a miracle all by itself.

By the time Dulce came we had our apartment set up. We had it all looking nice, the bedroom with the crib right across from where I slept so the baby crying didn't wake Skeeter. Even the kitchen was set up just right.

Dulce was a real good baby. While I was looking after her all day I kept making plans. One was that the other All Stars could do the DJ business in other places if they had somebody to pull it together. Skeeter could be their business manager if he thought about it.

I took Dulce in her stroller to the Chinese take-out

place and while we were waiting for the sweet-and-sour chicken and the butterfly shrimps I told her all about Skeeter and my new plan. "You think Daddy's going to like being a manager?"

She smiled.

poets
and
plumbers

"Noee, what are you going to do in the evenings if we start closing the shop earlier?" Abeni looked over the top of *Ebony*.

I knew what was behind the question. The hints had been coming in heavily casual comments, remarks meant to appear offhand, gentle words that crept into my sister's conversation and my mother's suggestion that we should all "get out more."

Abeni had broken up with Harrison but had started up a steady stream of e-mails with him as his career as an independent filmmaker grew. It was me they were worried about.

Other girls my age seemed to know what to do. They came to the shop thinking about how to look better, and told elaborate stories about the mating game. I watched little girls on the street, jumping rope or dancing, shaking their hips as if they were born knowing something that I didn't. I knew how the parts worked, that somehow when a man came near me, when he expressed an interest, I was supposed to know what to do, what to say. At the shop I had heard the talk, seen the smiles, the nods, the finger snaps. What I didn't know was why it didn't seem natural to me. I was seventeen and a lot of boys and a lot of men looked at me and offered up their word games but I didn't know how to play them.

Abeni was taking courses at City College, inching her way to a degree, but she was more interested in the beauty culture business than anything else. As much as I told myself that what I wanted to do was to spend my evenings reading, to talk about what was going on in the world, not just who was sleeping with who, I was beginning to feel that there was something wrong with me.

At times I was lonely, but it was a bearable loneliness, the way I imagined that a star, brilliant in a Milky Way of other stars, would be lonely.

Taking the creative writing course was not an answer so much as it was a refuge. I knew Abeni wanted me to go with her to some of the clubs downtown, but she let it drop when I said I was taking the course.

There were eleven people in the class. Six of them were older women who had taken the course before.

There was a young boy who wanted to write raps, an older man who had already published a detective novel, a severe-looking brother who wore a button that said BLACK MUSLIM and who wanted to reveal the Truth About the White Man, and Kyle Scott.

Kyle was six feet, maybe an inch more, and lean like some of the brothers who played basketball. When the instructor asked what we did he said he worked in the post office and was trying to get the money together to go to school full-time. He was serious-looking and I thought he really wanted to be a writer full-time but was shy about saying it. He also had a nice smile and a great voice. There was warmth in his voice, as if he cared about whatever it was he was saying.

One of the older women suggested we all stop for coffee after the class. Some of us did, including Kyle. We talked about films we had seen or hoped to see, the hot political topics, and books.

"Harlem has always had an amazing literary tradition," said one woman, a retired social worker. "I think storytelling is an important part of our heritage."

Kyle nodded. He knew a lot about the Harlem Renaissance and had read far more than I had. He didn't talk much during the meeting but what he said made sense. I didn't talk much, either, but I enjoyed hearing the others.

By the fourth week the after-class group had dwindled

to just some of the older ladies, the man who had been published, me, and Kyle. It was on a particularly warm March night, after our coffee group, when Kyle asked me where I worked.

"My family has a beauty shop on a Hundred and Forty-fifth. We live down the block from the shop."

"Do you walk uptown?"

"Sometimes," I said.

"If you're walking tonight, would you mind if I walked along?"

"Fine." I felt myself smiling, and now the embarrassment came in a sudden flush.

The night was warm and Malcolm X Boulevard was alive with the early-spring noises of Harlem. Music blared from the small shops or from radios set up on fire escapes outside the old tenements. Children who should have been busy doing homework were still in the streets and on 139th Street a man and woman were cooking sausages on a grill.

"You write well," Kyle said. "I liked the character studies you read tonight."

"Thank you."

As we walked I realized that I should have said something more to him, but everything I thought of seemed wrong. He had read some of his poetry and I thought it was quite good, far above the others in the class, but I wasn't sure how to criticize it and I didn't want to just say that I liked it.

He asked me if I went to school and I told him I was a senior at Wadleigh. He said he imagined that I had already selected a college.

"I'm not sure if I want to go to college," I said. "And you? You said you were saving money for school."

"Somewhere I can learn more about writing."

"Oh, I thought so," I said. "I mean . . . you write well."

"Uh, Noee, I have a poem I'd like you to see," Kyle said. "It wasn't something I wanted to read in class. Would you mind? You could bring it back next week."

"Why didn't you want to read it in class?"

"Well, it's kind of personal," Kyle said, nodding his head in self-agreement. "I was thinking about you during the week, wondering how I would describe you in words. The poem came from those thoughts."

"Oh." I hoped the flashing neon lights from Mable's Bar-B-Que covered up my flushing.

We said goodbye at my stoop and I took the poem and went in. Mama was sitting at the kitchen table playing solitaire in her slip. I kissed her as I pulled down the blind.

In my room I unfolded Kyle's poem and read it.

> *I wonder if the quiet moon*
> *Brilliant in the cold and distant sky*
> *Sees her own beauty*
> *On the jet black lake?*
> *Is she angered at the*

East-blowing cloud
Covering her perfect face
Or is she content
With the image in her heart?

I read the poem again and again until I had it memo-rized. What was he saying to me? Was he saying it to me? He had asked to walk me home. He had asked me to read his poem and said it had come of him thinking about me.

In bed I tried to read the day's paper, but my mind kept wandering back to the poem. I began to think of him. Foolishly. Like some schoolgirl wanting to have a crush on her hero. I tried to think of what I would say when I saw him in a week. Phrases came about the use of free verse and how the use of easy symbols, such as the moon, was very much overdone in poetry. Would I talk to Kyle like that? As if I didn't know the poem was about me?

I imagined us having a conversation. First it was at the coffee shop, and then it quickly changed to Central Park with the two of us sitting on a park bench. He was the shy one and I the one speaking boldly about the poems I had read and how I would have improved them. Kyle, handsome and reserved, nodding in quiet admiration at the wisdom of my remarks. Then, just as quickly, the imagined Kyle changed to Burn.

Burn would have turned away, would have ignored my carefully constructed sentences. I moved away from my imagination and into the safer realm of ordinary thought. It was still Burn I was thinking about. Perhaps he would have looked at me with those narrowed eyes. Perhaps his face would have hardened, scaring me somewhat. Perhaps he would have put his hand on my leg.

I thought of Kyle again. He had given me the poem. He had reached out to me. And I was afraid. There weren't that many eligible men in Harlem. Many of the ones my age were dropouts, not only from school but from life as well. The street corners were full of young guys who should have been working somewhere. Some of them already had police records. I didn't know what I was looking for, a black Prince Charming perhaps. Abeni said that I needed to figure out who I was first.

"If you want Prince Charming it means you're looking at yourself as some kind of secret princess," she said.

Was I looking at myself as a princess? I just knew I couldn't handle the easy-sex scene and I was a million miles away from Happily Ever After.

I wondered what my father would have said. "There's this boy," I would have said to him.

"Do you like him?" he would have asked.

"Yes," I would have said. "Yes."

The class was on Wednesday and I got there late after having to do two rinses in a row. Kyle wasn't there and I was grateful. I hadn't decided what I was going to say to him and thought of simply returning his poem without comment. Mrs. Baraf, the instructor, was reading from Chaucer in Old English to show us the poet's rhythm when the door opened and Kyle came in.

The chat in the coffee shop was about how one of the ladies had had a critique of her story from a magazine and was asked to resubmit it after a rewrite.

"To me that's as good as an acceptance," another lady said.

"It would be if they sent along a check with it," the rapper added.

We laughed about that and toasted the near success while I carefully avoided looking at Kyle. When the meeting was finally over and the group headed toward the 135th Street subway, I could feel Kyle's presence as he neared me.

"Was the poem interesting enough to merit another walk uptown?" he asked.

I mumbled. I'm good at mumbling. Sometimes I manage to shrug as I mumble. It must look stunning.

We started uptown again. The air was heavy, and cool. Occasionally there would be a few drops of rain in the warm wind, big splashy summer drops that warned of more rain to come. We walked three blocks in silence before he asked me what I thought of the poem.

"It's kind of romantic."

"That's what I had hoped for."

"Perhaps a little obvious, though," I added.

"Is that bad?"

I didn't know what he meant by that. I never knew what guys meant when they talked to me unless it was just about sex. A hundred men had leaned in my direction on the neighborhood street corners and mentioned what they would like to do to me in bed. I didn't like that, of course, and had learned to look the other way when I passed a man I didn't know. But now I couldn't tell if Kyle was talking about the poem or what he meant by the poem.

"The syllables are even," I said, numbly. "I don't mean that they have to be or anything."

We walked in a familiar silence. I had been quiet with boys before. Looking down, listening as my brain made Right Decisions. Outside of Ralph's barbershop there were two chess games going on and a small crowd of young people looking on. I liked that.

"Noee, can we go out sometime?"

"I'm very busy," I said. "This is my senior year and all. Plus I have to work in the shop. It's a family business."

"Did you know I was a good cook?" he asked.

"Cook?" I looked to see if he was kidding me.

"I was going to make a dinner for two this Saturday," he went on. "Something obviously romantic, most likely. I promise to write another poem for the occasion. Would you like to attend?"

"Come to your house for dinner?" My stupid heart was beating faster.

"For dinner and the poem," he said, taking my hand in his.

Somehow, against all my instincts, I got out a "yes." He lived downtown on 116th Street in one of those newly renovated places. At my stoop we exchanged phone numbers and he said he looked forward to seeing me on the weekend. Then he lifted my hand and kissed the ends of my fingertips.

It was so corny. I looked away as he released my hand and when I glanced up he was already backing away, headed back east toward the subway.

Thursday and Friday flew by. On Friday night I burned the back of a girl's neck. It wasn't anything serious but Mama was surprised. I thought that was the only thing that had gone wrong, but after we had closed Mama asked me if I was okay.

"You definitely had your mind someplace else tonight, girl," she said.

"I'm going to have dinner with this guy tomorrow and I'm thinking about calling it off," I said.

"Why, do you have to pay for it?" Abeni asked.

I told them about Kyle, how corny he was. "He gives me these poems and walks me home. He's just so . . . transparent," I said.

"All men are transparent," Mama said, "men like women. Do you like this guy?"

"Yeah, in a way," I said.

"Where's he taking you?" Abeni asked.

"He wants to cook for me."

Mama and Abeni asked a hundred questions. What did he look like? How did he dress? Did he have a job? They seemed almost more interested in him than I did.

Abeni loaned me a pink silk blouse to go with my burgundy slacks. She wanted me to wear her amethyst brooch but I didn't.

"This is not a first communion party." I was beginning to resent the attention.

"Chill, Noee, making people look good is our business," Abeni reminded me. "Have you forgotten?"

I hadn't forgotten. I just wanted to keep the date with Kyle in perspective. It wasn't a big thing, even if the only other date I had been on all year had been the day working with Burn on the cruise.

The buildings in Harlem were being renovated at a great rate. Places that had been abandoned were now being rehabbed and sold for outrageous amounts of money as both whites and blacks were moving into the area. Kyle's place had a security desk in the lobby with a round little man sitting behind it. He called Kyle to announce me. As the elevator went up to the seventh floor I felt my stomach tighten. When the elevator door opened Kyle was standing there with a big grin on his face. There was a middle-aged couple waiting for the elevator and they watched as Kyle kissed my hand. They smiled but I was embarrassed.

We made small talk with me sitting in Kyle's living room; he went in and out while he finished cooking. There were colored candles on the end tables and I imagined him seeing them in a magazine. Everything was nice, the apartment was spotless, but nothing exactly matched. I did like the framed prints on the wall.

"Elizabeth Catlett," he said. "They're knockoff prints but I like them."

Kyle served an avocado, tomato, and mozzarella salad that was very good. Then dinner consisted of chicken with sliced almonds, green beans, and baked potatoes. It wasn't fancy but it was good and I was relieved that he wasn't the world's greatest cook. Afterward I sat in an overstuffed chair. He sat on the couch.

As we talked I wondered if I should have sat on the couch with him. Would that have given him the wrong signal? Was I giving him the wrong signal by sitting in the single chair? I felt so awkward. There I was, glad to be sitting in his apartment, but not having a clue as to what to say or what to do. I could sense that he was trying to figure me out. He was trying to express his interest, and I was sitting there like a bump on a log.

"Do you think you could tolerate another poem?" he asked.

"Yes."

He had put the poem on the mantelpiece. He took it down, and asked me if he could read it to me. I said yes. He took a breath and started to read.

> *"I believe there are things around*
> *The corners of the world—*
> *Packaged delights, ripe fruits, sunset vistas*
> *Eager to dazzle the senses*
> *I believe there are loves just*
> *Beyond the moment, or the*
> *Moment just past that are in*
> *Grave danger of being missed*
> *I believe that, as I sit, wide-eyed*
> *And staring, there are so many*
> *Things to be missed.*

I didn't understand a word. The words jumped into my head and out before I could catch their meaning and all I was left with was the sound of his voice filling the silent spaces of the room.

"It's quite lovely," I said. And then, searching for more to say, "Do you ever use rhyme in your poems?"

He was sitting again. We were stringing words carefully. Minutes passed. An hour. I thought I saw him glance at the clock.

"Do you want to do the dishes?" I asked.

"No, well, all right," he said.

Kyle ran some water in the sink. When the water didn't go down he turned off the tap.

"It's stopped up again," he said. "I'll call the super on Monday."

"Again?"

"It's always a little stopped up—no matter," he said, turning away from the sink.

"Let's fix it," I said. "Do you have any tools?"

"I do, but . . ."

Kyle straightened up, trying to figure out what to say. Finally, he smiled and shook his head, saying something under his breath about it being the building's responsibility. I leaned against the sink—sinks were something I could do—knowing he would turn back.

"You actually think we can unstop the sink?" he asked. He stood in the doorway of the kitchen, his large frame filling most of it.

"Yeah, I actually think that."

Kyle shrugged and went to a cabinet and pulled out a gray toolbox. He looked under the sink and got on his knees.

"You need something to catch the trapped water," I said.

He looked up at me. "You do plumbing on the side?"

"Only around the house," I answered. "We own our place so we don't have a super to call. Can I try it?"

He started to raise an objection and I put a finger to his lips. He moved to one side and leaned against the refrigerator, watching me.

I put some newspaper on the floor to kneel on, then found a shallow basin and slipped it under the U trap. The wrench in Kyle's toolbox still had the original tag from the store. The nut on the bottom of the trap was tight, but I was able to wrestle it off and watched the water trickle into the basin. From the slowness of the water I figured it was either decayed food or a rag blocking the drain. It smelled terrible. The blockage turned out to be a dishrag, some food, and a fork.

All the while Kyle sat quietly watching me. Now it was he who felt awkward and me who had the confidence. I liked being close to him on the floor.

He didn't have a plumber's snake so I wasn't able to clean the pipe as thoroughly as I wanted to, but once I had replaced the nut and tightened it the sink drained properly.

"You're a wonder," he said, "and a mess."

I looked down at Abeni's blouse and saw an ugly dark mark. "Where's your bathroom?"

I went in, trying not to touch my filthy hands to the blouse again. There were the usual guest towel set and a roll of paper towels. I looked in the mirror and saw smudges on my cheek. I washed my hands and arms and dried them before taking off the blouse and wiping the grime and gook from my face and neck. My hand stung where I had scraped my knuckle.

It would have been a mistake to try to clean the blouse so I just slipped it back on. I used Kyle's pick to fix my hair. He was on the couch and I sat next to him.

"You're more impressive every minute," he said.

"Unstopping sinks is not very glamorous."

"I have a new CD I thought you might like to hear," he said, "Cesaria Evora with a band from Mali. Do you know her singing?"

I didn't know who he was talking about. For a moment I felt the same panic returning, the same self-consciousness that I always had with men. I decided to go with it. Kyle had left the poem on the mantel and I got up and got it. I brought it back to the couch and sat close to him.

"Read it again."

As he read, slower this time, I followed it on the page, moving his hands so I could see it as I leaned against him. The sound of his voice was warm, soothing in the stillness of the room, a stillness we had put together, like found art.

"Shall I call you Noee the Plumber from now on?"

"If you like."

He put his arm around me and we sat quietly. I imagined him trying to think of something clever to say, running lines through his head, testing them against his sense of poetry, and rejecting them. He wasn't holding me very firmly, which was good. Once he moved his hand up so that it just touched my breast and I moved it away.

I still felt as if there was something more I should have

been saying or doing, something I'm sure Abeni would have known to do. Perhaps everyone felt like this at some time in their life. I just sat with him, with his arm around me, feeling his chest rise as he breathed, the heat of his body warm against my cheek.

As we sat I couldn't turn my mind off no matter how I tried. Now I worried about how to negotiate leaving. Would he walk me home? How would he say goodbye? Would I let him kiss me? I wanted him to kiss me. But right now I wanted him to let me just be in the small moment that surrounded us, and not think about what it was I was supposed to do, or feel. I wondered if there would be a moon, fat and sassy, over the tenement roofs, daring me to be bolder than I thought I could be.

Maybe with Kyle, with his sweet poetry, it might be possible to be bold. I was as nervous as I always was with men but, for the first time in my life, I felt that I could try to figure it all out.

combat
zone

The small transport plane touched down harder than Corporal Curtis Mason thought it should and lumbered down the narrow runway. Through the port windows he could see the first rays of daylight streaking along the distant horizon. He grabbed the sling of the M-16 he had been carrying for the past few months and slung it over his shoulder. Across from him the two other Special Ops troops gathered their gear while trying to catch a glimpse of their new territory through the small windows. Curtis felt his stomach jump as he reminded himself that they were in Mazar-e-Sharif to replace soldiers who had returned in body bags.

"Gentlemen, welcome to northern Afghanistan." The heavyset sergeant who greeted them had a name tag that read "Duncan." "We will be bunked down a mere thirty-five miles from the border to Turkmenistan and the lovely Pyandzh River. Hope you all brought your water skis."

The jokes were always the same. How they would have all the comforts of home, how easy the mission would be, and, yes, try to avoid getting killed.

He had spent nearly seven months further south, outside of Kandahar, and had hoped for a rotation home when he, Timmy Moffett, and Jerry Maire were given temporary duty assignments to work in the northern area. None of them liked the assignment. Civilian Affairs specialists were to mingle with the locals and show them how good Americans really were and how great it would be for Afghanis to stumble into the twenty-first century. In return, or at least the way the theory worked, if the locals found out something that the military needed to know they would send the appropriate signals.

"How did the guys we're replacing get nailed?" Moffett, a tall white boy from French Lick, Indiana, broached the question first.

"Two by an IED," Duncan answered. "One by a sniper when he lit up a cigarette at night. It's careful time twenty-four/seven these days. We don't think it's the locals but some characters who have sneaked into the area and are trying to turn back the clock a few hundred years. We think we found the rag-heads who took out our boys. They're buried alongside the road."

The IEDs, improvised explosive devices, were what all of the Americans feared most. Left by the roadside, in trash bins, in stores and restaurants, they could go off at any time, triggered by remote control or trip wires. What they did to a human body was not to be thought about.

Curtis had already decided he didn't like Sergeant Duncan. He was too cocky, and "rag-head" sounded too much like "nigger."

Focus. He had to keep focused until he was rotated out. There was a rumor another Special Ops group, with their own CAs, would be brought into the area and then he would be on his way home. Home. Mazar-e-Sharif was nearly six thousand miles from 145th Street in Harlem.

He and Moffett were assigned to a squad, seven guys in a mix of sloppy uniforms. Some had grown beards. They all wore bandanas around their necks in case of sudden sandstorms and they all wore enough clothing, even in the oppressive heat, to conceal the body armor.

Mazar itself was typical of the towns he had seen in Afghanistan, barren by American standards, with people who could have drifted directly out of the pages of the Old Testament trying to scratch out a living as they made their way through the remnants of decades of war. Burnt-out vehicles, the bleached bones of animals, the pock-marked buildings that dotted the area alongside the road were grim reminders that these people had been suffering a long time. There was a crew of American engineers and Afghani workers building a new road that stretched northward toward the border. The Americans were pot-bellied, red-faced men who wiped at their faces continually, trying to keep the insects away. The thin Afghanis worked methodically. They did as much of the work by hand as they did with the bright yellow backhoes.

There were twenty-three men assigned as Civilian Affairs troops and Curtis saw only two blacks, a tall first lieutenant and a cute black sister who sometimes wore specialist-two insignia. He avoided both of them, but then the sister came up to him in the mess area and asked if she could sit.

"Sure."

"The Blue Mosque in town is what you have to see," she said. "And take pictures to show your kids if you have any."

"Don't have any."

"So, where you from?" Her face was dark and round, with eyes slightly lighter than Curtis thought they should have been. But it was her smile, warm and genuine, that seemed to reach out across the narrow table.

"Harlem," Curtis said. "You?"

"Philly," she had answered. "I got to say Philly because my time over here is too short to give you the whole formal name."

"I thought I would be on the way home this week," Curtis said. "But I'm looking around and noticing this is not Harlem."

"Time has a way of dragging over here."

"What do you do?" he asked.

"Same as you, Special Ops, building bridges. I'm supposed to deal with any women we come across. The only women I've dealt with so far are a few standing fifteen feet behind their men," she said. "And by the way, the name tag reads 'Sanders' and the missing part is 'Marian.' "

"Hey, Marian."

"Hey, Curtis," she said. "Got your name from the company clerk. You career?"

"No," he said. "Not career. Just counting my days to getting back into the world. You?"

"I'm thinking of what I want to take in my first semester at Spelman," Marian said. "Right now I'm thinking of 'Gracious Lady 101.' "

"Sounds good to me," Curtis said, returning her smile.

Marian finished the sandwich she had brought to the table and the container of apple juice. "I'm off. Got to have my nails done."

She was making light of her tour, something Curtis hadn't wanted to do. Not since he had seen his first dying man.

"Never get too easy with yourself," he remembered his grandfather saying. "You never know what's around the next corner."

Or the next patrol.

*   *   *

He was with Lieutenant Wayman, a couple of Civilian Affairs Ops, and two Afghani civilians doing a quick cover of a particularly irregular part of the road leading north from the camp to see if it could be traversed by heavy armor. They were in a GMV, a ground mobility vehicle, just over two clicks out of camp when a shot sounded from behind the vehicle. The local sitting next to Lieutenant Wayman stiffened in his seat and then slumped forward with a heavy sigh. Lieutenant Wayman slammed on the brake and twisted in his seat.

"Anybody got a direction on that?"

"No." Curtis, looking around frantically, felt his heart race. It was still an hour before night and they knew that the sniper who had knocked off the local could be up to a half-mile away. Worse, he could have any of them in his gun sights.

Wayman started up again and moved quickly down the road. Curtis suggested maybe they get off the road.

"Can't do it here," Wayman said. "They might have opened up to get us to go off the road onto an IED."

They drove the next fifteen miles of the patrol in under twenty-five minutes. The other local, an older man, somewhat browner than Curtis and wearing a loose shirt that came down over his thighs, patted the back of the man who had been shot. Curtis saw the way the man's arms flapped with the bouncing of the vehicle and knew he was dead.

Back at the camp they let some other locals take the body.

"They're Sunnis," Lieutenant Wayman said. "That's one of the reasons we're dealing with them up here. A lot of them have close ties to kinfolk in Iran. We're fighting this war and getting ready for the next."

Wayman's voice was low and flat. Curtis looked up at him and saw the tension in his face. He kept clenching his teeth between sentences. It was this war that was getting to the lieutenant, not the next.

Curtis shut him out. The guy killed had been less than eighteen inches from him. The sniper might have been aiming for him and missed.

The commanding officer of the Special Ops contingent increased the patrols. Rumors got around that the incident was a test, to see if the Americans were prepared for an attack. They made plans, trying to put them on paper while acting as casual as possible so that the locals wouldn't think they were getting nervous.

"I thought these people were going to be glad to see us," Moffett commented.

"The Afghanis don't have the theory down yet," Duncan answered with a smirk.

Two nights after the death on the road, Curtis woke in a cold sweat. For a moment he didn't know where he was, and then he remembered where he was and panicked because he didn't know where his weapon was. He knocked it out of the leather rifle holster he had bought and mounted on the side of his bunk and heard it clatter onto the plank floor. He retrieved it quickly, and listened in the darkness. Nothing, except for the slow breathing of Moffett in the nearby bunk.

He fell back across the bed, the M-16 tucked against his side. A glance at the clock's glow-in-the-dark numbers told him it was only a quarter to two.

He hadn't thought, either back home or at Fort Dix, that he would be scared. But seeing how easily death insinuated itself into the camps, how quietly it waited along the roads, how it jostled and pushed in the streets, had unnerved him.

Think about home, he thought. Focus on his mother, slightly overweight, in the kitchen. The kitchen that had needed painting for years. Focus on his father sitting at the end of the table drinking cold coffee in the mornings. Focus on being home, and away from the war.

Four days passed without incident and he began to breathe easier, or maybe he wasn't as conscious of his breathing as he had been. Marian had tried to talk to him again. In a way he thought she was light. She was always up in somebody's face chatting away. He wondered if she was giving anything up beside that marvelous smile. She was as friendly to the white soldiers as she was to him. He told himself that he didn't want to be friendly with her, or even to talk to her while he was in country.

June days were long but not too hot. The basic color of Afghanistan was light brown and in the summer months it was unbelievably dry. A thin layer of sandy earth covered everything so that the old buses, the mule-drawn carts, the mountains viewed through the haze and swirling dust, even the people were the same soft brown pastel.

The Afghanis were a decent sort, but he didn't like dealing with them. The CAs were supposed to treat the civilians with respect but they all knew that the suicide bombers and the faces behind the guns were the same color and mentality of the men they spoke to on street corners and in the small markets leading toward the city.

"If I was as desperate as some of these people I would go to the side that offered me my next meal," a Southern Special Ops troop drawled over breakfast. "I heard that two of them had a fight almost to the death over a first-aid kit."

A first-aid kit in a land where there were still thousands of mines buried throughout the countryside was no small matter. Curtis had never seen so many people with feet blown off, or walking with improvised canes. *Don't feel pity. Don't think about them. Shut out everything but getting home.*

He didn't think it was fair that he had been moved out of his company to a different command. Kandahar had been dangerous but they knew the city, and they knew where most of the bad guys would strike. It wouldn't be in the Green Zone, in the barracks area. In Kandahar you had to worry about patrols, but once you were back at the base you could relax with whatever diversion you could find, volleyball, pool, books.

"You'll get used to this place in a few days," Sergeant Duncan had told him. "Then one day your name comes up on the bulletin board and you're on that big silver bird headed toward the Promised Land."

Curtis wanted to believe him.

They were to travel due east to Kunduz, to a small settlement where the local well was supposed to be polluted. Moffett, Marian, an Afghani interpreter, and a medic rode with two would-be badasses from an airborne unit. They started at first light and pushed across the rugged terrain as fast as the cumbersome armored vehicle would go. By nine they were in what they thought would be the area and stopped on a small hill to check the maps.

The attackers, rising up from the nooks and crannies of the hills, were incredibly young.

"Back off! Back off!" The badass screamed as he sent a volley of automatic fire into the first of the masked figures.

Curtis felt himself lifting his M-16, felt its kick in his arms, felt the panic in his chest, and realized he wasn't aiming at anything. He was just shooting, just spewing death where it might land.

They backed down the hill, the automatic weapons firing in staccato bursts at the dark figures popping up like play targets along the hillside.

Now they were racing away. Now the firing stopped.

One of the badasses was cursing up a blue streak.

"They only got one of us, but we busted their rag-head asses!"

The one of us was Moffett. Curtis hadn't seen him hit, or heard him cry out. But there he was, curled in his seat, an ugly red stain covering the right side of his body.

There were things that Curtis knew. He knew the wrist position of a jumper from the three-point line. He knew the New York City transit system, where to switch from the A train to the 3 to get to a party scene in Brooklyn, but he didn't know death.

Moffett was about to fall to the floor of the vehicle. Curtis pulled him up and across his lap. He put his hand on his neck, feeling for a pulse. There was none.

He wanted to cry. He wanted to push Moffett's body away, to make it not happen, to make it not the guy he had drunk beers with at Fort Eustis and not the guy he had talked about world affairs with as they both dreamed about the end of the war and being alive.

They returned to the base and were debriefed by soldiers whose job it was to construct After Operations Reports. Curtis knew they would pretty it up, estimating how many of the insurgents had been killed, making heroes of the survivors. He'd seen it all before. He went to his bunk, lay down, and closed his eyes, telling himself that he wouldn't think about Moffett's death anymore, that he wouldn't relive his moments with him. He would shut out the war forever.

But then the girl, sitting on the edge of his bed, brought herself and the war back into his mind.

"I'm so afraid," she said.

"We're all afraid," Curtis said. There, he had said the words. "Things like this happen."

"Would it be terrible for you if we slept together tonight?" she asked.

He didn't want to sleep with her. He wanted to sleep alone with his being scared and his trembling and his cursing the world that he was in this miserable country in this miserable war and in any miserable country and in any miserable war when God should have known better.

"Yeah. Okay." His words.

He tried to forget about them but she came to his bunk and sat on the edge and held his hand in hers. Her eyes were tearful and she apologized for being so afraid, so needy.

"One of the reasons I joined the army," she said, "was that I didn't want to be abused anymore. I didn't want to be pushed around or told what I had to do or be used because I was a girl. Can you dig that?"

"No, not really," he answered.

"That's okay, too," she said. "But right now I need to be with somebody strong, somebody I think is going to understand where I'm coming from. I don't want to push up on you, but I need to be with somebody tonight. It's still okay with you?"

"Yeah."

An old blues tune rambled through his head. "I Needs to Be Be'd With." He thought Quincy Jones had recorded it. He wasn't sure, but he was sure that he wasn't somebody strong, or understanding where she was coming from.

They slept together. Their lean bodies curled in a tight knot, dark against dark, flesh against flesh, their bodies alive in the pitch-black night.

"We can win all the battles and still lose the war." The young major's fatigues were crisp, spotless. "What the enemy wants us to do—and don't be fooled into thinking otherwise—is to kick ass and leave a bunch of dead A-rab bodies lying around the villages so we look like the bad guys."

They had brought in two more squads of Special Forces troops to protect the CAs. It was just supposed to be a show of force, but a glance at the cocky, strutting guys showed that what they wanted to do was to throw their weight around.

When the major war had ended, when the Taliban had first been declared defeated and gone from Afghanistan, it had been a tug-of-war between the Civilian Affairs personnel, new on the scene, and what the CAs called the shooters. The CAs were trying, cautiously, to make friends with the locals while the shooters were more confident in their scopes, the body armor that made them look like some kind of giant insects, and the stubborn belief that they were immortal. They believed those bits of war and the headlines that said that the conflict was over, that it had all changed to a mopping-up operation and the education of the native populace. But as the victory wore on, as the need for the zippered body bags continued, it seemed more like a tug-of-war within each individual soldier and little to do with the Afghanis. It had become simply a matter of whether one had a better chance of staying alive by killing the natives or being friendly with them.

With the latest deaths the plan was to step up CA operations with the various groups in the area, especially concentrating on one particular warlord that army intelligence was trying to cultivate. The very fact that they were dealing with a warlord brought about a gut feeling of wrongness, but it was explained that dealing with outlaws, even with evil people, demonstrated the new army's flexibility.

Two CAs had been killed prior to Curtis's arrival and now Moffett. The Afghani's death wasn't mentioned. The mood in the camp had changed. Everyone was edgy. Tempers flared more quickly, there were more long letters to wherever home was, a few of the men prayed more. In the evenings the television sets were always tuned to the newscasts, looking for some indication that the final conquest had been complete and they would be withdrawing soon. Curtis was jumpy, too, but Marian had positively freaked.

All of the bravado, the easy chatter that had seemed so much a part of her, had disappeared. Now the smiles were forced. She hovered about him, touched him whenever she could, rubbing against him almost like a cat needing affection. She didn't come to his bed at nights and he was glad. He didn't want to be that close to anyone in this place.

She was still beautiful, always able to exude charm across the spaces between them. He liked looking at her, liked the way she moved, suggesting strength beneath the loose-fitting camouflage suit and high boots. She was also an invitation for him to come out of himself, to open up in a way that would allow her to come into his private world. To look for safety there.

Openness was not something Curtis was good at. Not during the war or at any time. He knew, knew because she pushed it into his face, knew because she rubbed it into his chest, that he was running from the idea of vulnerability and running from Marian.

Perhaps if the enemy had been clearer, if it had come

with white and gleaming horns protruding from a mass of dark hair, or if its eyes had gleamed like neon blood in the brightness of day, if it had howled at night so that he could follow the sound and know its form, things would have been easier for Curtis. He could have, perhaps, mustered up the courage and faced whatever death or injury he was threatened with. But that was not the face of the enemy. There were no horns, no red eyes shining from an evil scowl, no howl echoing from the silver desert moon.

The enemy was barefoot children playing in the wreckage of a Humvee still smelling of the corpses of its human cargo. The enemy was brown old men who had never seen America, who had never owned an atlas to find New York on a map, who had merely stumbled from the wars of their Old Testament lives into the wars of another time. What Curtis wanted to do, what he desperately wanted to do, was to shut it all away. Push away the morality, push away the fear, push everything away except the thought of going home.

Marian kept finding him. Kept probing into the uncertain edges of his consciousness.

Today she asked if he needed orange juice. "It'll help you to grow up into a real strong boy!" she said, the smile sliding through his cool. She was looking good in a white T-shirt over khaki shorts.

"How did you come to think the army was cool?" she asked him.

"Didn't like the scenes I was dealing with," he said,

looking away for the moment, ignoring his breathing faster because she was so close to him. "Guess that fits everybody who's regular army. I thought I could make up some scenes of my own and just stick myself in them. I did okay for a while."

"Yeah, me too," she said. "But Afghanistan ain't for a while. It's for the tour."

"We'll get though it," he said, surprising himself in admitting that getting through it was the only thing on his mind. Marian nodded silently. There wasn't a need for a lot of words.

The next assignment outside of the Mazar camp was to take bags of seed to a region near Baghlan.

"The local farmers know what to do with the seed, so all you need to do is to give it to them, sit around for a few hours and puff on their hookahs or whatever they call them, and get on back to base" was the informal order of the day. "It's a hundred and forty miles out, which should take three, maybe four hours, depending on the terrain you run into. Then it's four, maybe five hours back because you don't want to take the same route. You spend three hours with the locals. That's three hours minimum, and you get a full day's work for a full day's pay. Any questions?"

Curtis thought about Moffett. His grandfather had been a farmer and Moffett knew about things like the quality of soil.

"The earth's too poor over here," he had said. "You can't

grow anything. All they do here is bury the seeds and hope for the best."

The three Humvees pulled out on an overcast day but Curtis knew it wouldn't rain. The first one carried three CAs; one of them was Marian, along with the two-man crew. It was loaded with seed, food rations, and chocolate for the kids. The second was loaded with seed and fertilizer. Curtis was in the third with the crew and two Special Ops, including a skinny kid on the mounted squad gun.

They pulled out slowly, maneuvering their way through the concrete barriers that stopped easy passage through the base and that would have been used for shields in case they were attacked. They got the all clear from the southern gate detail and the first Humvee picked up speed as they hit the open road.

The distances between sites were hard to judge along the barren, empty roads. There were more changes of color in the northern part of the country, patches of green here and there, promising more than they delivered. Sometimes an old mosque, beautifully decorated, would rise majestically above the desert's constant dust swirls. Curtis found himself looking up at the sky a lot, glad to see something other than the brown of sand and stone.

Occasionally they would pass a group of houses, some as high as three stories, all still pockmarked from past wars. The Humvee crews spaced themselves precisely at six vehicle lengths, tightening up somewhat on curves and regaining their intervals on any straight road. There was chatter back and forth between the vehicles, and Curtis heard somebody talking about spending less time in the village. That was fine with him.

They were supposed to meet a group of farmers at an old marketplace. The market itself consisted of seven squat buildings, one with a Coca-Cola sign over Arabic writing. The men were sitting on makeshift chairs in a semicircle. There were two mules to carry off the bags of seed and an old converted vehicle that could have been a bus in its better days.

A group of children, bare-legged and ragged, stopped their games around an old well, undoubtedly dry, and waved. Curtis saw Marian waving toward the children. She was one of the first out of the trucks and was soon among the kids with a box full of goodies.

The men were the same as usual, bad teeth, signs of old wounds, one with a stump where his right leg should have been. They brought out papers to show.

"I think they're trying to show us where their farms are," one of the CAs said. "We're *not* taking this stuff to their farms so just let them unload it here."

The Americans looked over the papers, had one of the men make his mark on the requisition sheet, and indicated that they could start unloading the Humvees. Curtis resisted the urge to go over to the children and took a bag of fertilizer from the truck and cut it open so that the Afghani men could see the difference between that and the seeds. Several of them nodded and began talking among themselves.

The first shot hit the side of one of the trucks.

"We're fired on! We're fired on!" a sergeant screamed. "Mount up! Mount up!"

The men instinctively brought their rifles up and turned toward the buildings. Another shot whined past Curtis and one of the Special Ops opened up. He was shooting away from the village and Curtis turned and saw two dark heads in the distance. For a moment he tensed, then remembered to bring his rifle up to a sweep position as the men returned fire. There were cries behind him and he turned to see that two of the farmers had been shot. A woman, her black dress flapping as she ran, came screaming from the building toward the fallen men.

A shot, perhaps meant to be a warning, cut her legs from under her and she fell forward, sliding in the dirt.

Curtis looked for Marian and saw her disappear into a building with two of the children. He couldn't tell if she had been pulled in or if she was taking cover.

"Mount up! Mount up!" came the order.

The Humvee's machine gun was firing along a straight line some fifty yards away. All of the farmers were down, some with their hands over their heads in surrender, some wounded and twisting in pain.

The first Humvee was already pulling off. Curtis swung onto the second one and looked back for Marian. He didn't see her. The Humvee started a tight turn.

Curtis leaped off, stumbling forward for several steps as he tried to regain his balance.

"Get on the truck!" a voice barked.

Curtis raced toward the building he had seen Marian go into. The earth kicked up near his feet as shells hit the hard dirt. The outside of the building was bathed in sunlight, leaving the open door a patch of blackness. He jumped in, screaming as he did, trying to drown out the sound of his own fear, covering the desperation he felt. Something moved. He jumped to one side, tripping over something on the floor. He looked down. Marian!

He fired at whatever had moved and heard a grunt and a cry and a clattering of tin utensils as the dark figure turned into a human form. For a split second it had eyes and a mouth gaped open in agony. Then it was gone into the shadows.

He grabbed Marian's collar and pulled her toward the door with one hand, waving the M-16 with the other as he made his way backward out of the door into the sunlight.

"Stay down!" There was another soldier at his side. The Humvee had pulled up near the building and was hitting it with some heavy fire.

Curtis half-pushed, half-lifted Marian's still form toward the Humvee and she was pulled in. He jumped on, and a moment later the vehicle lurched forward and was speeding down the road.

Someone had taken Marian's helmet off and was pouring water on her face. At first she was still, then gasping for air.

"Call for Medivac! She's wounded!"

"Where are we?"

"Thirty-five clicks—I don't know—let them find us!"

"Mason! Good looking out, man. I didn't know she was missing! I didn't catch it!"

By the time the Medivac chopper located them they were only a mile from the base and they had decided that Marian's wound—she had been shot through her boot in the back of her leg—was more painful than serious. They drove her the rest of the way into the base.

It was late the next day before he went to the medical ward to see her. It had been twenty-four hours of reliving the events. Feeling the panic all over again, seeing the face of the person he had shot, undoubtedly killed, when he had burst into the building. He had thought of what he would say to Marian or, more clearly, what she would say to him. Would she tell him that she had run into the building? That they were protecting her there?

"Hi, how you doing?" she asked when he stopped near her bunk.

"I'm okay," he said. "How are you doing?"

She moved the cover off her leg. It was bandaged from

the knee halfway toward the ankle. "What do they say? The best wounds are the ones you live to talk about?"

"Something like that."

"Thanks for getting me out—they told me everything." She was crying.

"You really all right?"

"Sit down," she said.

Curtis sat down on the bed, watching Marian wince as she moved her leg to give him room. She took his hand and began to kiss it, to rub it against her cheek, even to wipe the tears away from her eyes.

"I don't know exactly what happened back there," he said.

"War happened," she said. "But we're not fighting now."

He leaned over and kissed her forehead, and then her lips. He felt her arms around his neck and felt her clinging to him. There were the tears, and the holding, and the feeling that he would never be strong enough to escape her arms, never strong enough to keep his heart away from her.

Later, he knew, there might come a time to talk about what had happened. They might talk, one day, of what the locals had been thinking, or even whoever it was who had fired at them. There might never be a complete understanding of what they had shared in those frantic moments, or what they had given up of themselves. Or what they had found.

about the author

walter dean myers is a poet, a novelist, a playwright, and a musician, as well as an avid collector of memorabilia. His books for young readers have received numerous awards, including two Newbery Honors, five Coretta Scott King Awards, four *Boston Globe–Horn Book* Honors, the Margaret A. Edwards Award, the first Michael L. Printz Award, the Alan Award, and the Virginia Hamilton Literary Award. *145th Street: Short Stories* was a *Boston Globe–Horn Book* Honor Book.

Walter Dean Myers grew up in New York City's Harlem.